The dentist stared long and hard at the boy, before uttering...

"Don't be scared, child..."

There is nothing designed to scare a person more than being told not to be scared.

"Let Mummy have a look at your teeth..."

Also by David Walliams

Grandpa's Great Escape

The Midnight Gang

Bad Dad

DEMON DENTIST

David Walliams

HARPER
An Imprint of HarperCollins*Publishers*

Demon Dentist

 For information address HarperCollins Children's Books, a division of HarperCollins Publishers, 195 Broadway, New York, NY 10007.
www.harpercollinschildrens.com

Library of Congress Control Number: 2015938900
ISBN 978-0-06-304524-8

---

20 21 22 23 24 PC/BRR 10 9 8 7 6 5 4 3 2 1

❖

Revised U.S. paperback edition, 2020

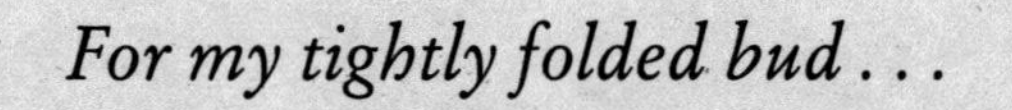

For my tightly folded bud . . .

BEWARE.
THIS IS A
HORROR STORY.

WITH QUITE
A LOT OF
MADE-UP WORDS.

Prologue

Darkness had come to the town. Strange things were happening in the dead of night. Children would put a tooth under their pillow at bedtime, excitedly waiting for the tooth fairy to leave a coin. In the morning they would wake up to find something unspeakable under there. A dead slug. A live spider. Hundreds and hundreds of earwigs creeping and crawling beneath their pillow. Or worse. Much worse...

Someone or something had come into their bedrooms in the hours of darkness, snatched the tooth and left a blood-curdling calling card behind.

Evil was at work.

But who or what was behind it?

How could they sneak into children's bedrooms without being seen?

And what could they possibly want with all those teeth...?

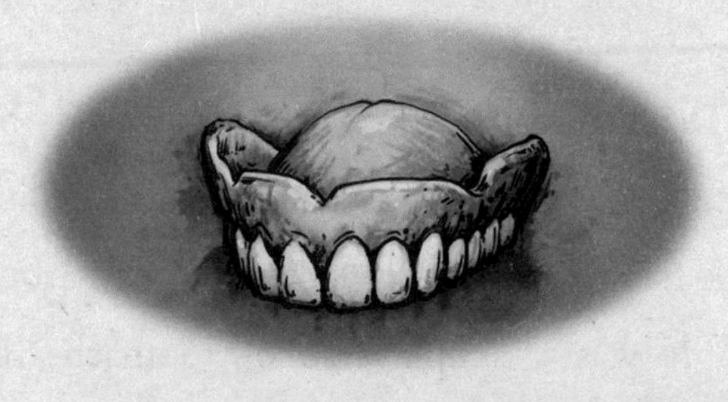

1

A Simple Case of Toothache

Alfie hated going to the dentist. As a result the boy's teeth were almost all yellow. The ones that weren't yellow were brown. They bore the stains of all the goodies that children love, but dentists hate. Sweets, fizzy drinks, chocolate. The teeth that were neither yellow nor brown simply weren't there anymore. They had fallen out. One had bitten into a toffee and stayed there. Assorted fruit-flavored chews had claimed others.

That's because this twelve-year-old boy hadn't gone to the dentist since he was very little.

Alfie's last visit was when he was around six. It was a simple case of toothache, but it ended in disaster. The dentist was an ancient man, Mr. Erstwhile. Despite his good intentions, Mr. Erstwhile should have retired many years before. The dentist looked like a tortoise, an old tortoise at that. He wore glasses so thick they made his eyes appear to be the size of tennis balls. Mr. Erstwhile told Alfie the tooth in question was rotten, a filling wouldn't save it, and unfortunately he had no option but to take it out.

The dentist yanked and yanked and yanked with his huge steel forceps. But the tooth wouldn't come. Mr. Erstwhile even rested his foot up on the chair by Alfie's head to lever himself against it to help wrench the wretched tooth out. Still it wouldn't come.

The ancient dentist then enlisted the help of his even older dental nurse. Miss Prig was instructed to hold on to him and tug as hard as she could. Even then the tooth wouldn't come.

Soon the hefty receptionist, Miss Veal, was asked to step into the room to help. Miss Veal weighed more than Mr. Erstwhile and Miss Prig put together. But even with all her ballast, the tooth wouldn't come.

Just then the dentist had an idea, and ordered Miss Prig to fetch some particularly thick dental floss. He carefully tied the floss around the forceps, and then looped it around Miss Veal's ample frame. The dentist then instructed his rotund receptionist to leap out of the window on the count of three. But even with all of Miss Veal's immense weight yanking on the boy's tooth, it still wouldn't come.

With poor young Alfie still lying in terror

on the dentist's chair, Mr. Erstwhile stepped into his waiting room to request reinforcements. The growing crowd of patients waiting to be seen were all called upon to assist. Young and old, fat and thin, the elderly dentist needed all the help he could get.

Nevertheless, even with a lengthy human chain and an army of yankers*, the tooth stayed well and truly put. By this time poor little Alfie was in great distress. The pain of having his tooth pulled out was a hundred times worse than the toothache. However, Mr. Erstwhile was determined to finish what he had started. Sweating profusely, the thirsty dentist took a large swig of mouthwash, and gripped on to the forceps as tightly as he could.

Finally, after what seemed like days, weeks, even months of yanking, Alfie heard a deafening

---

Made-up word* **ALERT

CCCCCCCCC
CCCCCCCCCCCC
RRRRRRRRRRR
UUUUUUUUU
UUUUUUUUU
UNNNNNNNNNN
NNNNNNNNNNNNN
CCCCCCCCHHHHHHH
HH!!!!!!!!!!!!!!!!!!!!!!!!!!!!!!

The dentist had gripped so hard he had crushed the tooth. It exploded into thousands of tiny fragments inside Alfie's mouth.

With the ordeal finally over, Mr. Erstwhile and all his helpers were lying in a tangled heap on the surgery floor.

"Well done, everyone!" he announced, as his assistant Miss Prig helped him to his feet. "Oh, that tooth was a stubborn little blighter!"

Just then Alfie realized something. He still had toothache.

The dentist had taken out the wrong tooth!

2

Believe

Alfie ran out of the dental surgery as fast as his little legs would carry him. That fateful afternoon the boy vowed that he would never ever go to the dentist's again. To this day he never had. Appointments had come and appointments had gone. Alfie had missed every single one. Over the years there had been a sackful of reminder letters from the dentist, but Alfie had hidden them all from his dad.

Alfie's was a family of two. Just him and his

father. The boy's mother had died giving birth to him. He had never known her. Sometimes he felt sad, as if he missed his mother, but then he would tell himself, how could he miss someone he had never met?

To hide the appointment letters from the dentist, the boy would silently drag a stool across the kitchen floor. Alfie was short for his age. He was, in fact, the second shortest kid at his school. So he would have to balance on his tiptoes on the stool to reach the top of the larder where he would hide the letters. There must have been a hundred letters buried up there by now, and Alfie knew his father couldn't reach them. That's because for many years Dad had been unwell, and had of late become confined to a wheelchair.

Before ill health forced him out of work, Dad was a coal miner. A great big bear of a man, he had loved working down the pit and providing for his beloved son. However, all those years he spent down the mine took a terrible toll on his lungs. Dad was a proud man, and didn't let on about his illness for many years. He worked harder and harder to dig more and more coal, even taking on extra shifts to help make ends meet. Meanwhile his breathing became shallower and shallower, until one afternoon he collapsed at the coal face. When Dad finally came round at the hospital the doctors told him he could never go down a mine again. Just one more lungful of coal dust could finish him off for good. As the years passed Dad's breathing worsened. Getting another job became impossible, and even everyday tasks, something as simple as tying a shoelace, grew to be a struggle. Soon Dad could only get around in a wheelchair.

With no mum or brothers or sisters, Alfie

had to care for his father alone. Besides having to go to school and do his homework, the boy would do all the shopping, all the cleaning, cook all the meals, and do all the washing up. Alfie never complained though. He loved his dad with all his heart.

Dad's body may have been broken, but his spirit wasn't. He had a great gift for telling stories. "Listen, pup...," he would begin.

Dad would often call his son that, which Alfie loved. The image it conjured up of a big soppy dog and a little puppy snuggling up together always made the boy feel safe and warm inside.

"Listen, pup...," Dad would say. "All you have to do is close your eyes, and believe..."

From their little bungalow Dad would take his son on all sorts of thrilling adventures. They would ride on magic carpets, dive under the oceans, even drive stakes through the hearts of vampires.

It was a multicolored world of make-believe, a million miles away from their black-and-white existence.

"Take me to the haunted house again, Daddy!" the boy would beg.

"Perhaps today, my pup, we will take a journey to the old haunted castle...!" Dad would tease.

"Please, please, please...," Alfie would say. Father and son would close their eyes and meet in their daydreams. Together they:

- Went out fishing for the day in Scotland and caught the Loch Ness Monster.
- Climbed the Himalayan Mountains and came face-to-face with the Abominable Snowman.
- Slew a huge fire-breathing dragon.
- Hid aboard a pirate ship and were forced to walk the plank as stowaways, only to be

saved by beautiful mermaids.

- Rubbed a magic lamp and met a genie who gave them three wishes each, although Dad gave all his wishes to his son.
- Rode on the back of Pegasus, the winged horse from Greek mythology.
- Climbed up a stalk to Giant Land and met an extremely hungry Cyclops whose perfect idea of a between-meals snack was a scrawny little twelve-year-old boy, so Dad had to save him.
- Became the first ever father and son team to successfully land on the moon in a homemade rocket.
- Were chased across the misty moors at night by a ferocious werewolf.

This was the world of the imagination. Anything was possible in Dad's and Alfie's adventures. Nothing could stop them. Nothing.

As Alfie grew older though, he found it harder and harder to see these things. As his dad spoke, the boy would open his eyes, become distracted, and begin to wish he could play computer games all night like the other kids at his new big school.

"Pup, just close your eyes and believe…," his dad would say. However, Alfie was beginning to think that now he was twelve, nearly thirteen, he was too old to believe in magic and myths and fantastical creatures.

He was about to find out how terribly wrong he was.

3

Whiter Than White

The whole of the lower school was gathered in the hall. The few hundred children were sitting in rows of chairs awaiting the guest speaker. No one interesting ever visited Alfie's school. On Prize-giving Day the guest of honor had been a man who made the cardboard for cornflake packets. The cornflake-cardboard man's speech was so mind-numbingly boring, even he fell asleep delivering it.

Today there was a talk from the town's new

dentist. It was to be a lecture about looking after your teeth. Not wildly exciting, but at least it meant they were all out of lessons for a while, thought Alfie. Not liking dentists, Alfie sat himself right in the back row, in his bedraggled school uniform. His shirt was once white but had long since gone gray. His jumper was full of holes. His blazer was torn in several places. His trousers were too short for him. Nevertheless, Alfie's father had taught him to wear his uniform with pride; the boy's frayed tie was always knotted absolutely perfectly.

Slumped next to Alfie was the only kid in the school shorter than him. A very little girl called Gabz. Seemingly shy, no one had heard her speak, despite her having been at the school now for a whole term. Most of the time Gabz hid behind her curtain of dreadlocks, not making eye contact with anyone.

When all the kids had finally stopped monkeying around and sat down, the headmaster took to the stage. If there was ever a competition to find the man most completely unsuited to being a headmaster, Mr. Grey would win first prize. Children scared him, teachers scared him, even his own reflection scared him. If his job didn't suit Mr. Grey, his surname definitely did. His shoes, his socks, his trousers, his belt, his shirt, his tie, his jacket, his hair, even his eyes were all shades of gray.

Mr. Grey had the whole gray color spectrum covered.

"C-c-c-come on now, settle d-d-d-down..."

Mr. Grey stammered when he was nervous. Nothing made him more nervous than having to speak in front of the whole school. Legend had it that one day the school inspectors visited and they actually found him hiding under his desk pretending to be a footstool.

"I s-s-said, s-s-s-settle d-d-d-d-d-d-own..."

If anything, the hum of the kids became louder. Just then Gabz stood on her chair and shouted at the top of her voice...

"COME ON! GIVE THE OLD FART A BREAK!!!"

It might not have been the most flattering choice of words, but the headmaster allowed himself a brief flicker of a smile as all the kids at last fell silent. Everyone looked at Gabz as she sat back down. After her outburst, the girl was now surrounded by the strange glow of celebrity.

"Good...," continued Mr. Grey, in his gray monotonous voice. "A bit less of that though, thank you, Gabriella. Now as a special treat for you, with a talk about looking after your teeth, here is the town's new dentist. P-p-please give a huge school welcome to the lovely Miss R-R-Root..."

As the headmaster scuttled off, there was a short burst of applause. Soon this was drowned out by a discordant squeaking sound from the very back of the hall. One by one the kids turned around. A lady was pushing a shiny metal trolley down through the parted sea of chairs. One of the wheels was catching on the wooden floor, and the high-pitched squeal was so brain-aching, some of the children even put their fingers in their ears. The sound was like someone scratching their fingernails down a blackboard.

The first thing you noticed about Miss Root was her teeth. She had the most dazzling white smile. Whiter than white. Like a fluorescent light. Her teeth were absolutely flawless. So flawless they couldn't possibly be real. The second thing you noticed about Miss Root was that she was impossibly tall. Her legs were so long and thin, it was like watching someone walk on stilts. She was dressed in a white laboratory coat, like the one a science teacher wears when it's time for an experiment. Underneath the coat, her white blouse was matched by a long white flowing skirt. As she passed, Alfie looked down and noticed a large splash of red on the toe of one of her shiny white high-heeled shoes.

Is it blood? thought Alfie.

Miss Root's hair was white-blonde, and arranged in a perfectly lacquered "do," usually only spotted on the heads of queens or prime ministers. The "do" was shaped much like a Mr. Whippy ice cream, minus the flake, of course.

In a certain light she looked very old. Her features were narrow and pointy, and her skin pale as snow. However, the dentist had painstakingly painted on so much makeup that it was impossible to tell how old she really was.

50?

90?

900?

Finally Miss Root reached the front of the hall. She turned around, and smiled. The low winter sun shone through the high windows and bounced off her teeth, causing the front few rows to cover their eyes.

"Good morning, children...!" she said brightly. The dentist spoke in a singsong manner, as if she were recounting a nursery rhyme. There was a collective groan from the kids at being spoken to as if they were toddlers.

"I said, *good morning, children...*," repeated the dentist, and she fixed them all with a powerful stare. So powerful that soon a hush descended upon the room. Then in unison all the assembled pupils said:

"Good morning."

"Let me introduce myself. I am your new dentist. My name is Miss Root, but I ask all my little patients like you to call me 'Mummy.' "

Alfie and Gabz shared a look of disbelief.

"So can I hear a great big 'Hello, Mummy'? After three! One, two, three..."

Miss Root mouthed the words silently as the children joined in.

"Hello, Mummy," they murmured.

"Excellent! Now I came to this town when a very unfortunate, indeed fatal, accident befell Mr. Erstwhile. The poor wretch must have fallen onto one of his own dental instruments. Oh, the irony! Of course there's no need to go into all the gory details, but suffice it to say, Mr. Erstwhile was found lying on the floor of his surgery in a huge pool of blood. The dental probe was embedded deep in his heart…"

A deafening silence descended on the hall. Alfie gulped. It was a horrifying image. Mr. Erstwhile may have been old and doddery, but could he really have accidentally stabbed himself in the heart?

"Mummy would like you all to give one minute's silence for Mr. Erstwhile. Now close your eyes, children. All of you. No peeping!"

Alfie didn't trust Miss Root enough to close his eyes. Nor did Gabz. Both screwed up their faces and squinted. From out of the tiny slits in his eyelids, Alfie spied something very strange. Instead of standing at the front with her own eyes closed, Miss Root tiptoed around the room inspecting all the children's teeth. When she finally reached Alfie's row at the back, the boy squeezed his eyes tightly shut for fear of getting into trouble. Miss Root must have lingered looking at his rotten set, as the boy could feel her cold breath on his face for a while before she tiptoed back to the front of the hall.

"And that's one minute!" the dentist announced. "Thank you, children, you can open your eyes..."

Alfie and Gabz looked at each other again. They were the only two kids who had witnessed Miss Root's peculiar behavior...

4

Blacker Than Black

"Of course, Mr. Erstwhile will be sadly missed," concluded Miss Root. "But as your new dentist I asked your wonderful headmaster if I could come here today. Mummy wanted to give you all a chance to get to know me, so I can welcome each and every one of you personally to my surgery. Now I am going to begin today's little talk with an incy-wincy question. Children, how many of you hate going to the dentist?"

All but one kid put their hand up. No one actually enjoyed going to the dentist. At best it was tolerated. The one boy who didn't put his hand up was too busy texting.

Alfie reached his hand in the air as high as he could.

"Oh! So many hands. Ha ha!" she laughed, though not in a way that suggested she found it funny. "So how many of you REALLY REALLY REALLY hate going to the dentist...?" incanted Miss Root in that singsong voice of hers.

Most of the hands stayed up, and Alfie actually rose out of his chair so his hand would be the highest. This boy was the king of really really really hating going to the dentist. After he had the wrong tooth pulled out, no one in the known universe hated going to the dentist more than Alfie.

"Ho ho ho!" said the dentist.

"Who on earth says 'Ho ho ho'?" whispered Alfie to Gabz.

"So lame!" replied the little girl.

"Well, Mummy is here today to tell you there is absolutely nothing to be scared of..." The words danced in the air as she spoke. If her tone of voice was meant to sound reassuring, it didn't. It sounded the opposite of reassuring. It was in fact decidedly unnonreassuring*.

"Now I need a volunteer, hands up...!" said the dentist.

All those little hands that had been up were now well and truly down. To avoid any confusion, Alfie shot his hands down to his feet. Any lower and they would be underground. He wanted there to be a less than zero chance that he would be picked.

"Nobody...?" asked Miss Root.

Even the swots and show-offs kept deadly silent.

Made-up word* **ALERT

"Come on, children, I don't bite!" The dentist smiled and flashed her blindingly white teeth.

"Who hasn't been to the dentist for a very very long time…?" she purred.

The pupils started whispering to each other and looking around. Soon hundreds of pairs of eyes were glaring at Alfie. Everyone at school had at some point noticed his teeth. They were so bad, they might as well have been a tourist attraction. They could even have their own café and gift shop.

The dentist followed the children's gaze and fixed her eyes on Alfie.

"Oh yes, I thought it might be you..." Miss Root's long, thin, gnarled finger pointed straight at him. "You, boy. Come to Mummy…"

When Alfie's shaking legs finally propelled him to the front of the hall, he looked into the dentist's eyes for the first time. Miss Root's eyes were black. Blacker than oil. **Blacker than coal. Blacker than the blackest black.**

In short, they were black.

The dentist stared long and hard at the boy, before uttering...

"Don't be scared, child..."

There is nothing designed to scare a person more than being told not to be scared.

"Let Mummy have a little look at your teeth..."

Alfie kept his mouth firmly shut.

"Open wide, there's a good boy..."

Suddenly Alfie felt as if he couldn't help doing exactly what the dentist told him. He opened his mouth, and she peered inside.

"Oh...," moaned the woman in pleasure. "Your teeth are absolutely abhorrent..."

The whole of the lower school laughed at him.

"HA HA HA HA
HA HA HA HA HA
HA HA HA HA HA
HA HA HA HA HA
HA HA HA HA HA
HA HA HA HA HA
HA HA HA HA HA
HA HA HA HA HA
HA HA HA HA HA
HA HA HA HA HA
HA HA HA HA HA
HA HA HA HA HA
HA HA HA...!!!"

Except two children—Gabz, who looked on with sadness at the cruelty, and Texting Boy, who was still texting and had missed everything.

"Oh dear, oh dear. What is your name, child...?" inquired the dentist.

"Alfie, M-M-Miss...," the boy spluttered.

"Call me Mummy..."

There was no way he was ever going to call anyone that, least of all her.

"Alfie what...?" continued Miss Root.

"Alfie Griffith."

"Well, young Alfie Griffith, you simply must make an appointment to come and see me at my surgery very soon..."

Alfie shuddered at the thought. He had vowed never to go anywhere near another dentist as long as he lived.

"Do you like presents, child...?"

Like all kids, the boy loved presents.

"Y-y-yes...," he replied.

"Well, Mummy's got a little present for you. For being such a good boy today, here—

have a free tube of my own special brand of toothpaste..."

From the trolley, Miss Root picked up a thick white tube with the word "MUMMY'S" emblazoned in big red letters on the side.

The slogan "Mummy loves your teeth" was inscribed in smaller black letters under that.

"And one of my special toothbrushes. Do you prefer hard or soft bristles, Alfie Griffith...?"

The boy had had the same toothbrush all his life. He had no idea whether it once had been hard or soft. Right now there was only one lonely bristle left. It was virtually bristleless*.

"I don't mind..."

"I'll give you a nice soft one, then...," announced Miss Root.

A gleaming white "MUMMY'S" toothbrush was produced from the trolley. The bristles on

---

Made-up word* **ALERT

the end were sharp and wiry. Alfie ran his finger along them and winced. It was like stroking a porcupine.

Holding the brush and tube in his hands, Alfie looked like a tearful child you might see at the zoo who has been made to face their fear of spiders by being given a huge, hairy, highly poisonous tarantula to hold.

"Alfie, we shall meet again..."

No, we won't! thought Alfie.

"Oh yes, we will...," she whispered. It was as if the dentist could hear his thoughts...

5

Special Sweeties

"Now be a good boy and pop back to your seat…!" ordered Miss Root. Alfie did what he was told. Not wanting to catch anyone's eyes for fear of further humiliation, he put his head down as he trudged back to his seat.

"Now, children…," continued the lady, "who else would like a present? I have some free sweeties…?"

Hundreds of hands shot up, and soon the hall was humming with the chattering of excited children.

"But don't sweets rot your teeth?" shouted out Gabz.

Miss Root glared at her, then smiled. "Oh, aren't you a feisty one? What's your name, child...?"

The girl hesitated, but eventually said, "Gabz..."

"Well, of course, young Gabriella is right. Normally sweeties do rot your teeth. But not these ones. No! Mummy's sweeties are special. All my sweeties are completely sugar-free, so you can eat as many as you like..." From under the trolley she pulled out a tray, and whisked a white sheet off the top of it. Underneath was a huge pile of brightly colored goodies. There were chocolates and chocolates and more chocolates. Toffees and fudge. Sucky sweets and chewy sweets. Fruity ones and minty ones. Melt in your mouth sweets. Crunchy sweets. Fizzy sweets. Explosive sweets.

"Come on, children. Don't be scared. Come and help yourselves to Mummy's special sweeties..."

In an instant, hundreds of children surged forward and started eagerly grabbing huge handfuls of sweets. As many as they grabbed, and the greedy little boys and girls were stuffing their faces and pockets, there seemed to be more. And more. And more.

"Take as many as you like!" Miss Root called over the din. "I can always magic up some more...!"

Alfie noticed Gabz was sitting stock-still in her seat.

"Are you not gonna get any?" asked Alfie.

Gabz shook her head. "No."

"Why not?"

"Haven't you ever heard the tale about the brother and sister who go into the woods and find the house made of sweets...?"

Alfie was surprised that the little girl's imagination had run away with her like this. "Hansel and Gretel? Yes, of course, everyone has, but that's just a stupid fairy story."

Gabz turned her head and fixed him with a stare.

"It's not stupid. And just because it's a fairy story doesn't mean it never happened...," she said, before turning her gaze back to the dentist who was smiling broadly with those impossibly white teeth of hers, as the kids filled all their pockets with sweets. Strangely, however many the children took, there were more and more and more filling the tray.

Along the rows, just one boy stayed glued to his chair. It was Texting Boy. He was still texting.

*

On his way home from school that afternoon, Alfie wanted to dispose of the presents Miss Root had given him as quickly as possible. He didn't trust that lady one bit. There was something deeply disturbing about her. That splash of red on her shoe, the creep around the hall in the minute's silence for the dead dentist, and those sugar-free sweets that never ran out were just too good to be true. So when Alfie crossed the bridge over the canal as he always did on his way to and from school, he stopped. He pulled the toothbrush and toothpaste out of his blazer pocket. He examined the label, "MUMMY'S." It was such a comforting brand name. How could you not trust anything called "MUMMY'S"?

The boy unscrewed the lid of the tube. Immediately some sticky yellow gunk, the color of pus, snaked out of the end. It smelled rank, like warm sick. A small glob of it fell to the ground. It hissed and fizzed as it bore its way through the stone bridge like acid.

What is in that toothpaste? thought Alfie. Just then he noticed the paste was still oozing out of the tube. It was moving dangerously close to his fingers. A smidgen of it landed on his skin, and instantly he could feel it burning.

"Ow!" screamed the boy. He quickly threw the tube into the canal below. It plopped into the water, and he watched as the tube sank to the bottom, the paste still snaking out. Then Alfie noticed he still had the hard wire toothbrush Miss Root had given him in his other hand. The bristles looked like they would scratch your teeth away, rather than clean them. So he threw the brush in the canal too.

As Alfie took a couple of paces to continue on his journey home, a strange sound stopped him in his tracks. Looking back he saw that beneath the bridge, the water in the canal was boiling and bubbling. It was like a mini volcano erupting. The boy watched in horror as a school of dead fish plopped to the surface and floated there. As he peered down at the water, a gaggle of kids from his school passed him, laughing and joking, their mouths full of "MUMMY'S" chocolates and toffees and fruit chews. Every single child looked like they couldn't be happier, greedily munching and crunching and scrunching them.

If that's what her toothpaste does, thought Alfie, *what on earth is in those special sweets of hers…?*

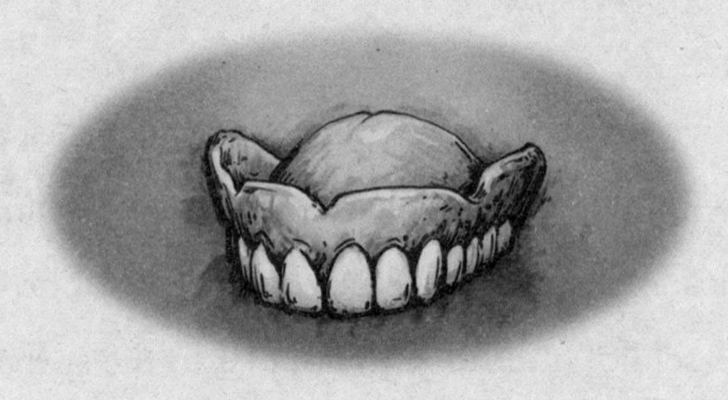

6

The Intruder

"You must be Alfred," boomed a voice when he walked in the front door of his little bungalow, which squatted in an estate on the edge of town.

"Who are you?" demanded the boy. Alfie was very protective of his dad and didn't like seeing strangers in the bungalow.

A flamboyantly dressed lady had plonked herself down in the living room with Dad. Her ample frame was taking up more than one place on the worn and torn sofa.

The riot of color in her mismatched outfit (yellow scarf, pink stripy leggings, green top, and electric-blue shiny plastic coat) looked decidedly out of place in the small, gray room. In fact, it would have looked out of place anywhere.

Dad was sitting in his wheelchair in the corner of the room where he always was, a frayed tartan blanket covering his knees. It was cold in the bungalow. The central heating had been cut off a few winters ago. In truth, their little home was falling to pieces. Since Dad had been confined to a wheelchair, the bungalow had fallen into a state of disrepair. Despite Alfie's best efforts, water poured in through the roof when it rained. Cracks had appeared in most of the windows, and mold was creeping up the walls all the way to the ceiling.

"Oh, son, this is..." Dad took a loud shallow breath. "...Winnie. She's a social worker."

"A what?" asked Alfie, still staring rather rudely at the intruder.

"No need to be worried about me, young man, ha ha!" proclaimed the big jolly lady, as she plumped up a cushion and placed it behind Dad's back. "I'm here from the council. Social workers like me just want to help..."

"We don't need any help, thank you," said Alfie. "I look after my father better than anyone else could, don't I, Dad?"

Dad smiled at his son, but didn't say anything.

"I am sure you do!" replied Winnie with a smile. "By the way, it's very nice to meet you, young man," she said, reaching out one of her podgy hands with fingers like bejeweled sausages. Alfie just stared at it.

"Shake her hand, son. Be a good boy...," implored Dad.

Alfie reluctantly let his little hand meet hers.

The social worker gripped it tight and shook it so vigorously, the boy thought his poor arm would be yanked out of its socket. The multicolored plastic bracelets that adorned her wrists rattled loudly as she did so.

"Now, young Alfred, could I trouble you for a cup of tea?" bellowed Winnie.

"Yes, a pot of tea would be lovely, thanks, son," prompted Dad. "Then we can all sit down together and have a good talk."

"I can't have coffee, it goes right through me! Ha ha!" added the social worker.

Alfie stared at this intruder as he backed out of the living room to make the tea. Father and son always shared a pot of tea when Alfie returned home from school. He would lay out a tray with two cups. It had been just two cups for as long as he could remember.

One thing the boy had learned from his

father was that however poor they were, they should still take great pride in life's simple pleasures. So when Alfie made the tea he would try his hardest to make everything just so. As the kettle was boiling, he fetched a little chipped teapot with the lid missing and placed it on a tray he had liberated from the school cafeteria. Then he took two cups out of the cupboard. There were only two cups in the house, so Alfie had to think on his feet. Eventually he found an eggcup, and put it on the tray. That would do for his mouthful of tea. The milk jug was really a moonlighting gravy boat Alfie had bought in a charity-shop sale. Last but not least, the boy took out a cracked plate, and arranged three crumbling out-of-date chocolate biscuits on it. The local newsagent had given Alfie a free packet one day when the boy looked particularly hungry.

With a proud smile on his face Alfie entered the living room carrying the tray. Carefully he placed it down on the coffee table (well, it was really just an upturned cardboard box, but he and Dad called it the coffee table).

"I have heard so much about you from your father, young Alfred," said Winnie, spraying biscuit crumbs all over the boy and the carpet and even as far away as the curtains as she spoke. She took a large and noisy slurp of her tea from her cup, and washed the remainder of the biscuit down her throat.

"Aah!" she sighed, smacking her bright-pink painted lips together. "That's better. I am soooo looking forward to getting to know..."

As she spoke Alfie tried to smile, and sipped some tea from his eggcup, feeling somehow like a tiny giant. Winnie peered at the boy. She slid along the sofa, and her big fat face came close to his, like a hippopotamus inspecting a little bird that has landed on its nose. "Oh, my word! Look at the boy's teet!"

"My what?" said Alfie.

"Teet!"

"My teet?" replied Alfie, confused.

"Yes, boy...," said the social worker in a frustrated tone. "YOUR TEET!"

"I think Winnie means your teeth...," ventured Dad.

"Yes, that's what I said!" implored the lady. "TEET! T, E, E, T, H, TEET!"

"All right, all right. What about my teet, I mean teeth?" asked Alfie, before quickly closing his mouth to hide them. He knew he wasn't going to be asked to star in a toothpaste advert anytime soon, but they hadn't all fallen out. Yet.

"No no no, that won't do. Oh, my word!

That won't do at all. As your social worker, the first thing I am going to do for you..."

"Yes...?" gulped the boy, guessing what might be coming.

"...is make you an appointment with the dentist!"

7

Secrets

Alfie gave his father a look, imploring him to throw this annoying lady out. Now. However, Dad turned to face her, squinting a little at the riot of color. "I think that's a very good idea, Winnie. I don't want any more of his teeth falling out before his thirteenth birthday."

"Ha ha! No!" laughed Winnie. "We don't want that. A quick trip to the dentist will sort the boy out!"

Without asking, she helped herself to her

third chocolate biscuit. It was the last one on the plate. Even though it had a hint of mold, Alfie had been eyeing up that biscuit for the last ten minutes. That was all he was going to eat this evening for his dinner. The woman wolfed it down whole, and took another deafening slurp of her tea.

"SSSSLLLLLLLUU UUUURRRRRPPPPPP!!!!"

She smacked her lips together again, and then let out another sigh.

"Aaaaaahhhhhh!!!!!!!"

It was only the second time she had done the slurpyaah* routine in front of him, but Alfie couldn't hide how deeply annoying he found it.

Dad broke the uncomfortable silence. "Oh, it's so nice to have a visitor, isn't it, Alfie?"

The boy said nothing.

Made-up word* **ALERT

Winnie slurped and aahed again before inquiring, "Have you got any more of these yummy biscuits, ha ha?" She laughed at the end of her own sentences, in that irritating way jolly people often do.

"Yes," said Dad. "We should have another biscuit in the tin, shouldn't we, Alfie?"

Still the boy sat in silence, staring at this multicolored munching machine.

"Well...?" prompted Dad. "Go and bring another biscuit for the nice lady."

"Another chocolate one if you have it please, ha ha!" added Winnie brightly. "Naughty, I know! Have to watch my figure! But I do love choccy biccies!"

Slowly Alfie stood up and trudged to the kitchen. He knew there was one last chocolate biscuit in the tin, but he had been saving that for their dinner tomorrow night. Half each. As he passed the scratched and mottled mirror in the hall, Alfie paused for a moment. He needed to pluck the larger fragments of spit-sodden biscuit that had sprayed out of the social worker's mouth from his hair.

"You must be very proud of him, Mr. Griffit," said Winnie. Alfie could hear them from the hall.

"It's Griffith..."

"That's what I said! Griffit."

"Griffith...," repeated Dad.

"Yes!" said the woman in an exasperated tone. "G, R, I, F, F, I, T, H. Griffit!"

"Well, um, yes of course I'm very proud of my pup," wheezed Dad. Long sentences sometimes got the better of him.

"Your pup...?"

"Yes, that's what I call him sometimes."

"I see."

"Over the years he's looked after me so well.

His whole life he has been looking after me. But…" Dad's voice lowered to nearly a whisper now, "I didn't tell him but I had a fall last week while he was at school. I didn't want to worry him."

"Mmm, yes. I can understand that."

Alfie shifted his weight so he was standing nearer the door. The boy listened intently as the grown-ups talked.

"I became short of breath and I just blacked out. I fell out of my wheelchair. Smacked straight on to the bathroom floor. I was rushed to hospital in an ambulance. The doctors did a load of tests…"

"Oh, yes…?" Winnie sounded very worried now.

"Well, they, um…" Dad was struggling to find the words.

"Take your time, Mr. Griffit."

"Well, the doctors told me my breathing was getting worse and worse. And fast…"

"Oh no!" gasped Winnie.

The boy could hear his dad crying. It was heartbreaking.

"Here, Mr. Griffit, have a tissue...," said the social worker softly.

Alfie took a deep inhalation of breath. Hearing his dad cry made him want to cry. But the proud man was fighting it, and sniffing back up the tears.

"We Griffiths are strong. Always have been. I worked down that mine for twenty years. As my dad did before me, and his dad before him. But I am a very ill man. And my poor little pup can't cope all on his own..."

"Very sensible of you, Mr. Griffit," replied Winnie. "I am glad you finally decided to call the council. I just wish you had sooner. And remember, I am here to help you, and your son..."

Alfie stood frozen to the spot. Dad had a

habit of keeping bad news from him. The rising debts, the TV and the fridge being repossessed, Dad's worsening health. Alfie felt he was always the last to know.

Indeed, despite their closeness, there were plenty of chapters in Alfie's life that he kept from his father. The boy had his secrets too.

That the bigger boys would bully him at school for "dressing like a tramp."

The detention Alfie received for not doing his homework when he had been too busy cleaning the bungalow the night before and hadn't had time.

When he was caught "bunking off" by the headmaster. Actually he had had to leave school early to make it to the next town before the shops closed to collect a new wheel for his father's wheelchair.

Alfie felt his dad had more than enough

things to worry about without worrying about him too.

But overhearing the conversation from the living room, try as he might not to, the boy finally had to give in to his tears. He was a Griffith too. Strong and proud. But his tears had beaten him. Warm, salty drops ran down the boy's face. Despite everything, Alfie had always believed that one day his dad would get better. Now he had to face the truth.

8

Teet

"Alfie?" called Dad from the living room. "What about that biscuit for our new friend Winnie?"

Hastily, Alfie tiptoed back across the hall to the kitchen, and busied himself there. He had heard something he was never meant to hear. And now he had to hide it.

"I'll go and check on him, Mr. Griffit," announced the lady.

"By the way, Winnie, it's Griffith," said Dad.

"That's what I said," corrected Winnie. "Griffit."

She thundered down the hallway. Alfie didn't want this stranger to see him cry. He hated anyone seeing him upset. Growing up without a mum, Alfie's life had been touched with more sadness than most children's. As a result, he had learned to hide his feelings. To bury them somewhere deep within where no one could see. His heart was a fortress.

Alfie hastily dabbed his eyes with the sleeve of his blazer, before attempting to wipe away the tears that had run down to the end of his nose.

"Now, young Alfred, have you found any more biscuits?" inquired Winnie. The boy had his back to her, and didn't turn around. He hoped that in a few more moments all trace of his tears would be gone, and his red and blotchy face would have returned to normal.

Winnie could sense something was wrong. "Alfred? Alfred? Are you all right, young man?"

The boy hastily grabbed the scratched-up old biscuit tin from the larder. Still not turning to face her, he passed it over roughly.

"There you go. Eat the last one, why don't you?!"

Winnie slowly shook her head, then her eyes were drawn to the mountain of letters on top of the larder behind Alfie.

"And what are all these...?" she asked.

"All what?" replied the boy. Alfie turned round, and in a panic realized she meant all the dental appointment letters he had been hiding from his father for the past few years.

"That's just rubbish," he lied.

"Well, if it's just rubbish, let me help you put it in the bin." Winnie was a wise old bird. She reached up her hand to grab the letters.

Before Alfie could say anything, her eyes started flickering through the pages. Soon his secret was out.

"Well, who would have thought it! They're all letters from the dentist! Oh dear, Alfred, you haven't been for years!" proclaimed the social worker. "Now I know a lot of children under my care are scared of the dentist, but trust me..."

Alfie snatched the letters out of her hand. "Stop poking your nose where it doesn't belong!" he barked. "I love my dad and I look after him better than anyone else could. Better than you. Better than anyone. So why don't you just walk out that door and never come back? Just leave us alone!"

Winnie looked at Alfie, waiting for his white-hot anger to cool. Slowly, her head tilted to one side. In her job as a social worker she had met many troubled children over the years, but none quite as spirited as this boy. She took a breath, before saying, "Please, Alfred, believe me, I am here to help you and your dad. I know it's not going to be easy for you to accept that. I know you probably hate me right now..."

The boy's silence was telling.

"But who knows, Alfred, in time you may come to like me. One day we might even be friends..."

Alfie scoffed at the thought.

"Now, young man, why don't we sit down and have a little talk...?"

The boy couldn't control his rage at this woman any longer.

"There is nothing to talk to YOU about!" he shouted, before pushing past her out of the cramped kitchen.

As he dashed along the hallway to his

bedroom, Winnie called after him.

"Please, Alfred…," she implored.

But the boy simply ignored her, slammed his bedroom door shut behind him and locked it. Alfie slumped down on his bed. He shut his eyes tight in frustration. Just then he heard a gentle tapping on the door.

TAP TAP TAP.

Even the way she knocked on the door was annoying to him.

"Alfred?" she whispered. "It's Winnie!"

Alfie said nothing.

"Just to say, I am off now," said Winnie, pretending nothing was wrong. "But I will call the dentist first thing tomorrow morning about your teet. I've heard a very nice lady has just taken over, by the name of Miss Root. Bub-bye!"

Alfie gulped. Not Miss Root. Anyone but Miss Root…

9

Tell No One

The next morning at school Alfie opened his locker to find a note that had been slipped under the door. It had been made from letters cut out of a newspaper, and there was no name at the bottom. It read: *Boiler room. Lunch time. Tell NO ONE.*

The boiler room was deep within the vaults of the school. It was strictly out of bounds to all children. Alfie looked behind him to check no one saw him, as he sneaked down the spiral staircase that led to it from the playground.

Keep out!...read the sign. Slowly Alfie turned the handle and pushed open the heavy door. It creaked. It was dark inside, and the hiss and gurgle of the giant boiler was so loud no one upstairs could hear you. Not even if you screamed. Realizing this suddenly, Alfie felt a shadow of fear passing over him.

He was afraid. Perhaps being lured down here was some kind of trap. From behind the boiler, out stepped a figure.

A short figure with dreadlocks.

"Gabz!" said Alfie, as he breathed a sigh of relief. "Why are we meeting down here? We could get into big trouble if a teacher found us."

"Keep your voice down!" hushed the girl. "You don't know who could be listening. Now, quickly, wedge that old blackboard up against the door so no one can come in..."

Alfie did what he was told. Gabz double-checked the door was secure, and then rolled out a huge piece of paper she was carrying on the damp and dirty floor. They knelt down to study it. Soon Alfie realized this was a giant map of the town. Gabz had drawn it in some detail, and had written notes in colored pens by certain homes. Urgently she pointed out places on the map as she spoke:

"Two weeks ago. November 10th. Jack Brown, a wasps' nest. November 12th. Lily Candy, cat poo. Same night. Eddie Larter, a dirty old verruca sock..."

Alfie was bemused. "What is all this...?" he asked.

"November 13th. A Friday. That was a busy night. Crisscrossed all over town. Rian Skinner, a dead adder.

"Twin sisters Jessie and Nell Godwin, a giant

scab. Origin unknown. Might not have been human.

"Hardeep Singh, flying ants' eggs. Woke up to his bedroom buzzing with thousands of them…

"I don't understand," said Alfie.

"And last night it got me. My tooth fell out, well, after I waggled it for weeks, so I put it under my pillow as I always do. What do you think I woke up to find?"

"I, er, um, don't know."

"A bat's wing!"

"No!"

"Yes. Still flapping. Must have just been ripped off the poor beast."

Alfie couldn't believe what he was hearing. The girl was gathering pace now. There was no stopping her.

"So I started asking around the school

first thing this morning, and realized it was happening all over town. Kids here, here, here and here...," said Gabz, as she pointed out a number of houses or flats on the map, "...were all targeted last night. And the calling cards got worse. Much worse. A badger's paw, a snail that had had its shell pulled off, hundreds of centipedes creeping and crawling under some poor girl's pillow, a filthy, sticking plaster, sodden with pus..."

The boy couldn't help but shudder. "That's disgusting!"

"Whatever's happening, this is just the beginning..."

"Who is doing this?" asked Alfie.

The little girl shook her head. Her dreadlocks followed soon after. "Nobody knows. None of the kids I have spoken to saw or heard a thing. First they knew of it was when they woke up in the morning expecting to find a shiny new coin."

"And you didn't see anything last night?"

"Nothing," replied Gabz. "I lock my bedroom door at night, and I live on the seventeenth floor of a block of flats, so tell me, how did they get in…?"

Alfie thought for a moment. "Well. They couldn't have done…"

"They did," replied Gabz firmly. For a moment she looked lost in thought. "Maybe they flew in…"

Alfie couldn't help but laugh. As far as he was concerned the little girl's imagination was now running away with her.

"Come on, Gabz! That's impossible!"

Gabz looked at him. "Nothing's impossible, Alfie."

Still he was not convinced. "Maybe we

should take this map to the headmaster…"

Now it was the girl's turn to laugh. "Mr. Grey?" she asked in a mocking tone. "He's useless. Besides, he allowed that demon of a dentist into the school."

Alfie's mind was whirring now.

"You don't think Miss Root could be involved somehow?"

Gabz thought for a moment. "No. How could she? All these different houses all over town in one night. It's just not possible for just one person…"

"No, I suppose not…"

"But there is something very strange about her…," said Gabz, as she stared off into space.

"Whatever you do, don't try her 'MUMMY'S' toothpaste. It burns through stone!"

"What?" asked the girl. This was a new piece of the puzzle.

"Yes. I dropped a tiny bit of it and it went right through the bridge. I threw it into the canal and it killed all the fish."

"Glad I wasn't stupid enough to take a tube...," proclaimed Gabz.

Alfie didn't like that one bit. "Gabz, Miss Root made me take it!"

"Whatever!" The girl smiled. It was clear she enjoyed winding Alfie up.

"Look, between us we've got a lot of evidence here," said Alfie. "I say we forget the headmaster. Go straight to the police..."

10

Urgent Police Business

"So, kiddy winkies, let me get this straight...," sighed PC Plank, "we are talking about some evil, flying, tooth-snatching monster?"

The policeman was more used to dealing with speeding tickets and hedge disputes between neighbors. Unsurprisingly, he was not the least bit convinced by the children's story. It was straight after school, and Alfie and Gabz had raced down to the police station as fast as their legs could carry them. Now they were sitting in a brightly lit interview room with a not-so-bright policeman.

"I never said it was definitely one hundred percent a monster!" replied the girl.

Plank shook his head wearily. "But it could be a monster?"

She nodded.

"And nobody has seen it. Oh yes, and it only comes out at night!" PC Plank scoffed.

"That's right," replied Gabz, trying to put a brave face on it. Quickly she unrolled her map. "Look, officer. Every one of these kids has woken up with something horrible under their pillow..."

The policeman studied the map for a moment, but he couldn't be swayed.

"Probably just their older brother or sister's idea of a joke!" replied Plank eventually.

"Kind of a sick joke, don't you think?" asked Alfie forcefully.

"Well, I, er...I suppose it is, er, a little strong...," spluttered the policeman.

The boy was sure he had PC Plank on the ropes. Now all he had to do was deliver the knockout punch. "And we both think it might be something to do with the new dentist, Miss Root. She came to our school yesterday and gave me a free tube of her special toothpaste..."

"What of it?" replied PC Plank.

"It burned through stone."

The policeman narrowed his eyes and furrowed his brow. This detail of their story definitely interested him. "Did you bring this toothpaste with you today, lad?"

Sheepishly, Alfie shook his head. "No, I, er... I threw it in the canal."

Plank looked decidedly unimpressed. "Littering. That's a criminal offense. Could do you for that!"

"But...," protested Alfie.

"Well, lad, if you and your girlfriend don't mind..."

Girlfriend?! Alfie was horrified at the thought. He'd never had a girlfriend, and was still at the age where he thought girls were yucky. Completely and utterly yuckety*.

"She's not my girlfriend!" he protested.

"As if I would go out with him!" chimed in Gabz.

"All right, all right, if you and your 'friend' don't mind, I have some urgent police business to attend to."

"What's more urgent than this?!" demanded Gabz.

The policeman looked aggrieved. He wasn't used to being spoken to like that.

"If you must know, I have an eighty-year-old woman waiting in the cell. She was

---

Made-up word* **ALERT

apprehended in the supermarket with a Scotch egg stuffed down her tights."

"Oh, excuse me!" said Gabz mockingly. "I had no idea a master criminal was in our midst."

Alfie smirked. He loved how cheeky his new friend could be. Predictably, PC Plank didn't see the funny side. In fact, he was infuriated. So infuriated that he stood up sharply and shouted,

"OUT!"

The pair stood outside the police station in the freezing cold. Alfie tried to console Gabz, who looked utterly dejected.

"Come on, Gabz, you can't blame him," said Alfie. "I mean, it does all sound really hard to believe..."

It was only the late afternoon, but it was already becoming dark. A wicked winter wind whipped through the air as the little girl looked up to the sky.

"They'll strike tonight," said Gabz. She gazed at the black clouds rolling overhead. "I just know it. Somewhere in this town a child will wake up screaming..."

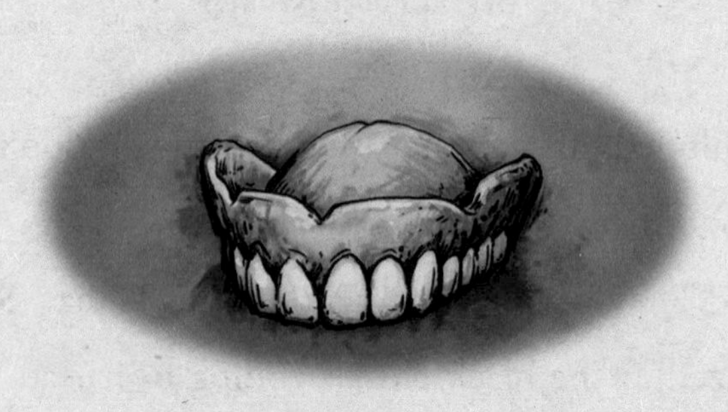

11

The Plan

"You're late, son...," called Dad from the living room, as Alfie walked in the front door of the bungalow.

"Oh, I was, er, just at chess club...," replied Alfie. It wasn't the smartest lie, as he barely knew how to play draughts, let alone chess, but he didn't want his father to worry. Then, entering the living room, Alfie saw that SHE was back.

Winnie.

Fussing over Dad's blanket.

"Good news, young Alfred!" she announced.

"What's that?" said the boy. He was hoping Winnie was going to say she was moving abroad.

"I've got you an appointment with the dentist!" she said proudly.

Alfie shuddered.

"Good news, isn't it, son?" said Dad.

"I spoke to Miss Root on the phone this morning," said Winnie. "She told me she remembered meeting you at your school yesterday. Anyways, she said she was all booked up with patients, but as your teet are so bad she could squeeze you in tomorrow at two!"

Tomorrow was a Wednesday and Alfie was of course meant to be at school, in a double maths lesson, to be precise. The boy hated maths, but **double** maths, even **triple** maths, **QUADRUPLE** maths or **INFINITY** maths would be preferable to going to have his teeth poked, prodded, or even pulled out. Especially by that woman. Alfie loathed everything about maths, every single little bit of it—the times tables, equations, algebra—but those instruments of torture were far less painful than any dentist's.

"Thanks so much, Winnie," lied Alfie.

"How will you get there?" asked Dad.

"Don't worry, I can easily get the bus there myself from school tomorrow afternoon."

The town's bus service had a long-standing reputation for being unreliable. Of course, Alfie had no intention of going anywhere near the dentist, and with the bus service being what it was, he would have a long list of possible excuses as to why he didn't make his appointment:

- I waited and waited but the bus never turned up (an oldie but a goodie).
- I got on the wrong bus, one which was

actually being used by a motorcycle display team to jump over.

- The fattest man in the world stepped onto the bus and it toppled over onto its side.
- The bus was delayed for hours as it stopped at the zoo and a waddle of penguins tried to get on, but none of them had the right change and the driver became quite irate.
- A gang of bank robbers hijacked the bus and diverted it to Mexico.
- The driver went the wrong way and the bus got stuck under a low bridge. A group of scientists then had to miniaturize it so it could get on its way, and of course this took time, as they had to invent the miniaturization machine first.
- Next-door's dog ate the bus (this works better for homework).
- The bus was in fact a Transformer, a robot

in disguise. So the journey to the dentist was delayed as it fought with other Transformers for control of the universe. Also there were some roadworks.

- The bus got a flat tire, so we needed the world's strongest man to lift up the bus so the wheel could be changed. As none of the passengers knew who the world's strongest man was, we had to organize our own "World's Strongest Man" competition at the side of the road, and the series of challenges to determine the winner took several days.
- The bus was sucked into a space-time vortex and I was propelled billions of years into the future to when aliens rule the earth (this one only to be used as a very last resort).

However, Winnie eyed the boy with suspicion. She had dealt with all sorts of difficult children in her many years as a social worker. The town was full of kids like Alfie, who would lie and cheat their way out of having their nits or their ear wax or their verrucas or their teeth seen to. Quick as a flash, she replied, "No no no, Alfred. You don't get no bus..."

"No...?" asked Alfie.

"No. I will take you there myself on my moped."

"Thank you so much, Winnie," said Dad.

"All part of the service, Mr. Griffit."

The social worker expounded on her plan:

She would collect Alfie from school on her moped at 1:30 p.m. The journey was only fifteen minutes, so there should be absolutely no chance he would be late. In fact, most likely he would be early.

When they arrived at the dentist's, Winnie would take him upstairs herself. That way there would be no opportunity for the boy to take an unscheduled detour to the local sweet shop.

Next, as Miss Root poked and prodded Alfie's teeth, Winnie would wait, and book the boy a follow-up appointment.

Finally, she would drop him off back at school. He wouldn't even have to miss all of double maths!

It was so well thought through. How could it fail?

Alfie watched at the window as the social worker, looking like a giant tropical fish, chugged off down the road on her little red moped. The machine made a rather stuttering **tut-tut-tut** sound as she motored away. Winnie was quite a menace on the road. She swerved around parked cars and leaped over a speed bump before bringing the moped up into a wheelie as she disappeared out of view.

*

"So, my pup...," said Dad, as father and son sat in the living room by candlelight later that night. The electricity company had cut them off years ago. "Are you ready for tonight's adventure...?"

"Yes, Dad," he replied dutifully.

In truth, the boy wasn't. Alfie had bigger things on his mind than going on some imaginary voyage.

"So close your eyes, and believe...," implored Dad. Alfie sighed, and reluctantly half-closed his eyes. While the other boys at school were watching movies in 3D or playing the latest computer games, he was forced to sit in the dark with his father.

"Let's believe we are in an old castle, sitting around a huge, round, wooden table. We are wearing heavy suits of armor. There are long swords by our sides. We are knights. And there are another ten knights seated around us. It is the time of King Arthur and we are two of the Knights of the Round Table. Now you take over, son..."

Alfie's mind had wandered. There was so much buzzing around his brain right now... the terrifying goings-on in the town that Gabz had uncovered...the arrival of the busy-body social worker...the dental appointment with the deeply creepy Miss Root. So although Alfie had heard what his father had said, he hadn't listened.

"Okay, erm, well, we're knights right, so erm...I dunno..."

Dad opened his eyes, and saw that Alfie's were open too.

"What's the matter, son?"

"Nothing, Dad. Sorry, I just have a lot of schoolwork on at the moment. Got some big tests next term..."

The candlelight flickered in the dark, but there was enough light to see that Dad was upset. He reached out for his son's hand.

"Pup, you'd tell me if there was something wrong, wouldn't you?"

"Of course," said Alfie, as he pulled his hand away. His mind was racing. There was no way he was going to go anywhere near that dental surgery. Alfie needed a counterplan. And fast.

12

The Counterplan

Every morning before school, Alfie had to get up super-early. This was because, besides getting himself ready for the day, he had to look after his father too. So after putting on his school uniform, he helped Dad get washed and dressed. Next he made them both some breakfast. This morning there was nothing left in the larder save for a solitary stale crust of bread. The boy gave his dad the bigger half, but Dad swapped the plates when Alfie had his back turned so his son could have it.

Before Alfie knew it, he was running late.

"Now remember, Winnie will pick you up from the school gates at one thirty to take you to the dentist," said Dad.

"How could I forget...?" mooched the boy.

"She's a good woman. She's even called the school for me so they know all about it."

"That's kind of her," replied Alfie, in a stilted tone.

"Now don't be late."

"Don't worry, Dad, I'll be there," lied the boy. Alfie kissed his dad on the forehead as he did every morning, and left for school.

Unable to sleep last night, Alfie's mind had whirred for hours formulating a counterplan. It was simple. Devilishly simple.

He would hide.

It was a three-point plan:

1. At 1:29 p.m., Alfie would ask to be excused from double maths to go to the dentist.

2. Then instead of walking to the school gates to meet Winnie, he would conceal himself somewhere. The school was vast and there had to be hundreds of great hiding places. The store cupboard, under a pile of lost property, even behind the atlases in the library. Anywhere where this meddling woman wouldn't be able to find him.

3. Finally, he would stay hidden until the bell signaling the end of school rang, then simply join the throng of pupils leaving for home.

"Psst, Alfie..."

The boy looked around the school playground but he couldn't see who was whispering to him.

"Psst...Behind the bins..."

It was first thing in the morning and the whole open space was bustling with children arriving at school. Hesitantly, Alfie circled the bins, and breathed a sigh of relief when he saw that the voice belonged to his newest and littlest friend.

“Oh, hi, Gabz,” said Alfie.

“Last night. Another thirteen reported attacks!”

“Wow!” Alfie was gobsmacked.

“Kids found all sorts under their pillows…”

“Like what?”

“A puppy’s tail sliced clean off…a hairy wart…an electric eel still wriggling…And this morning, haven’t you noticed anything different?” said the little girl.

“About what?”

“The kids. Look at them…”

Alfie peered out from behind the bins, observing his fellow pupils. At first glance he didn’t notice anything particularly different.

“I don’t know…,” said the boy.

"I thought you weren't like the others. I thought you were smart..."

Alfie was determined to go back up in the girl's estimation. Now he looked closer and noticed the kids were much quieter than usual, many of them holding their jaws in pain.

"Toothache!" proclaimed the boy.

"Bingo! We got there!" sighed Gabz.

"It must have been all the sweets Root was giving out..."

"You don't say," she retorted, in a sarcastic tone.

Alfie was beginning to tire of being spoken to like he was a complete dummy. "Please just shut up for a moment. I am beginning to find you really annoying."

Alfie gathered his thoughts. "So obviously those sweets can't be sugar-free. They must be absolutely packed with sugar. But why is Root doing this? Just to get new patients...?"

"Or some kind of sick and twisted joke?" mused Gabz.

Alfie suddenly remembered. "You won't believe this, but my social worker got me an appointment to see Root this afternoon..."

A broad smile crossed the little girl's face. "That's brilliant!"

"What?" said Alfie, incredulous.

"You can have a look around her surgery for clues. See if there's anything to connect her to all the tooth snatching that's been going on."

Alfie couldn't believe what he was hearing. "Are you crazy? That woman frightens me. I am not going anywhere near her surgery. Who knows what she might do...?"

"Scaredy cat."

Alfie looked down at Gabz. He couldn't believe he had been called a "scaredy cat" by:

A girl.

Who was only eleven.

And at least a foot shorter than him.

"Say that again!" demanded Alfie.

Gabz wasn't easily intimidated. "Scaredy cat scaredy cat scaredy cat," she taunted.

"Hey, Miss Marple! You're the one who's desperate to find out all about her. Why don't you go?!" sneered Alfie.

Gabz fixed him with a stare. "Maybe I will...," she said. And with that the little girl turned, flicked her dreadlocks, and made her way into the main school building.

The school day passed painfully slowly for Alfie. Lessons seemed to stretch on for hours. The boy was waiting and waiting for double maths, when he could put his three-point counterplan into action. There was no way he was going to Miss Root's surgery and letting that woman loose on his teeth. Alfie didn't care one bit if that made him a "scaredy cat."

Finally the clock clicked into position. It was 1:29 p.m.

Right on cue, Alfie put up his hand in the middle of a particularly devilish piece of algebra, and asked to be excused from class.

His maths teacher, Mr. Wu, had been informed of the dentist appointment by the school secretary, and let him go.

"Jolly good. I do think it's high time you had your teeth seen to, Griffith...," announced the teacher, to sniggers from the rest of the class.

Alfie said nothing. He stood up, collected his books, and left the classroom.

Boom! The counterplan was running like clockwork.

All he had to do now was find somewhere to hide. And fast.

As Alfie walked he surreptitiously checked

the handles on the cleaning cupboard doors. Darn. Locked. As he passed classrooms, he ducked a little under the glass in the doors to avoid the darting eyes of suspicious teachers.

Heading upward, he passed a window on the central staircase and peered out. Through the grimy glass, Alfie looked past the empty playground to the huge school gates. The unmistakable and unmissable figure of Winnie was standing out in the rain, her little red moped by her side. The woman had a big orange anorak on that was blustering in the winter wind. It gave her the appearance of a tent that was about to tear free of its pegs and flap off high into the sky. For a moment, Alfie felt a pang of guilt that the social worker was out there in the cold waiting for him. *She is only trying to help, isn't she?* he thought, before another thought crossed his mind...*No, she's just an interfering old bag.*

Silently he watched as Winnie checked the time, then looked up at the school. Alfie ducked his head. Had she seen him? He couldn't be sure.

Running up the stairs, the boy continued his desperate search for somewhere to hide. The classrooms were all in use, the pottery room was locked, and going all the way down to the boiler room right now was far too risky. Then somewhere deep in the belly of the school he heard a sound. A sound that Alfie couldn't possibly have planned, counterplanned or even countercounterplanned* for. The *Tut-tut-tut* of Winnie's moped going along the corridor…

Made-up word* **ALERT

13

Impro!

Alfie belted past a sign that read: *NO RUNNING IN THE CORRIDOR.*

He was becoming breathless now, and a sense of panic was descending on him. How could he outrun a moped? Even one with a very heavy load? The noise of the bike's engine was becoming louder and louder. Winnie was getting closer and closer. Alfie tiptoed to the central staircase, and hid behind the balustrade. From high up on the third floor, he looked down to see where she was heading…

Tut-tut-tutting along the bottom corridor was the little red moped. The social worker's legs were astride it. The bike was advancing slowly, Winnie's sandals skimming the floor as she peered into all the classrooms to see if she could spot her prey. Even from this height, Alfie could tell Winnie was fuming. No one likes having to wait outside in the wind and rain. Now the social worker's face was curled up like she was chewing on a stinging nettle.

Alfie kept dead still for a moment. Winnie might detect any sudden movements.

After a patrol up and down the lower corridor, the social worker stood up on her moped. She circled around the bottom of the stairs a few times to gain speed, then suddenly, with a sharp twist of the throttle she mounted the first step.

Alfie leaped up from behind the balustrade, and as he did so, Winnie spotted him.

"ALFRED!"

she shouted as the moped bounced up the stairs.

"ALFRED! COME BACK HERE, BOY!"

Alfie was running, but he didn't know where to. He darted down another corridor, bouncing off the walls as his legs carried him faster than his mind could direct him. The map of the school plotted out in his head from all that time trudging between lessons was now alerting him to something. He was reaching a dead end.

The hum of the moped's engine was getting louder. Now Alfie was at the end of a corridor, pinned against a large bank of lockers. Winnie had reached the top floor and was hurtling toward him.

He leaped to his left. Darn. The stupid language lab door was locked. Still the moped was coming straight toward him. He leaped to the right and turned the handle.

He put his weight against the door and burst into the room. Alfie found himself in the middle of a drama class...

"And go with it! Impro!" cried the teacher.

Mr. Snood taught drama. He was a bald and bespectacled man who always wore a black polo neck jumper, black jeans, and black shoes. If he stood next to the black curtain in the assembly hall, it looked like there was a giant boiled egg floating through the air. Snood lived and breathed drama. Drama was his love. Drama was his life. Drama was his drama. Snood taught his subject with a ferocious sincerity.

Alfie found all that pretending to be a tree business in Snood's classes acutely embarrassing. Most of the pupils did. In fact, as Alfie burst through the door, all the kids were loitering in the middle of the classroom looking like they would rather be anywhere else than here. They were reluctantly trying to improvise (or "impro" as Snood called it) a scene based around the end of the world. This was always Snood's favorite starting point for any "impro"—the world ending.

"A giant meteor is about to hit the earth. Impro!" is how the floating egg would start most of his classes. Then Snood would take his chair and spin it around rather dramatically (how else?). With it facing the wrong way, he would sit with his short legs astride it. From there the drama teacher would watch intently as his pupils shuffled to and fro mumbling something about a giant meteor hitting the earth but really just praying for an actual meteor to hit the earth to save them from the embarrassment.

"I said, 'IMPRO!'" exclaimed Snood.

"I'm not doing drama today, sir...," uttered Alfie.

"That doesn't matter, boy...," announced Mr. Snood in his deep, rich voice. It sounded as rich as chocolate mousse. "You have become part of the scene. So a giant meteor is about to hit the earth and wipe out all human, animal, and plant life! IMPRO!"

"Erm...," said Alfie. He couldn't think of a single thing to say, but could hear the moped stuttering just outside the room.

"IMPRO!" implored Mr. Snood.

"Erm, um, mmm, bad news about the whole giant meteor thing hitting the earth," spluttered Alfie, "but on the upside the pizzas I ordered are here..."

Just then Winnie's moped crashed through the door. Even Snood looked a little taken aback at this, but with the improvisation growing by the moment, this was no time to stop.

"IMPRO!"

"What?" replied Winnie, fixing Alfie in her sights as she skidded to a halt.

"Tell us what flavors of pizzas you have!" exclaimed Snood.

"I ain't no pizza delivery service, you fool. I'm a social worker..."

"Now, class," Snood turned to his pupils, "what this lady has done here is...anybody? No? She's swapped roles midway through an impro. As I have always said, that's an IMPRO NO-NO!"

"I am here to get this boy to the dentist!" exclaimed Winnie.

"What I would say now, and I know the first rule of impro is...anybody? No? Never stop an impro. ANOTHER

IMPRO NO-NO. But I do feel passionately, what with a meteor hitting the earth and pizzas just having been delivered (which by the way was a very skillful piece of 'impro-ing*,' huge congrats, Alfie, you may well want your final meal to come with a free garlic bread), that adding a dentist appointment into the mix is just too much. I'm sorry, but it's AN IMPRO on AN IMPRO on AN IMPRO and as such is a

HUGE IMPRO NO-NO!"

Winnie paused for a second, her whole body wobbling as the moped engine reverberated. She fixed Mr. Snood with a steely gaze.

"I don't know who you are, but please stop talking out of your **bum bum!**" Then she turned her focus to Alfie. "Now, you get

---

Made-up word* **ALERT

on this here moped at once!"

The boy stood motionless on the spot for a moment.

"I like this though, building tension, sense of drama, theater at its best...will he get on the moped or not...?" whispered the teacher to his class.

Suddenly Alfie pushed a chair into the path of the moped and fled out of the room. Winnie swerved around it in hot pursuit.

"Let's go where the impro takes us! Come on, my actors. This is impro on the move!"

With that, Snood stood, punched his fist in the air triumphantly and led his utterly bemused students out of the room. They chased after Winnie, who chased after Alfie, as he ran back down the corridor.

The boy turned the corner and ran smack into his headmaster coming the other way.

"Now come on...," said Mr. Grey, trying

his hardest to sound authoritative, but failing. "What does the sign say?"

"Toilets?" offered up Alfie.

"The other one!"

"Oh, 'No running in the corridor,' sir."

"Thank you. You nearly knocked me clean over!"

"Sorry, sir."

"You could have had someone's eye out."

Alfie wasn't sure this was true, teachers tended to say this a lot. In their minds, just about anything (a stray football, a bag left in the wrong place, even late homework) could have an eye out.

However, this wasn't the time to argue.

"Yes, of course, sorry, sir," agreed Alfie.

"Now be on your way, boy," said the headmaster. A proud smile spread across his face. At last he had done something head-masterishly*.

"Thank you, sir."

Made-up word* **ALERT

Alfie walked off as quickly as he could without breaking into a run. Mr. Grey straightened his gray tie, combed his fingers through his gray hair and continued on his way with a renewed sense of self-importance.

However, as he turned the corner, he screamed…

"AAAAAAAAAA RRRRRRRRRRGG GGGHHHHH!"

Winnie was flying toward the headmaster on her moped.

"Out of the way, you fool!" she shouted.

Just in time, Mr. Grey leaped against the wall.

"Excuse me, madam!" the headmaster called after her. "No riding of mopeds or any kind of two-wheeled motor vehicles in school corridors, please!"

Winnie didn't look back. She barely heard him, such was the roar of the engine. The headmaster stood and watched Winnie disappear off down the corridor, shaking his head and tutting to himself. Just then he was knocked over by the drama teacher and run over by thirty of his pupils.

As Mr. Snood passed, he commented, "Very powerful trampled underfoot acting, Headmaster! Huge congrats!"

14

Balls

Alfie galloped around the next corner and tripped over a schoolbag. With both his eyes still intact, he fell toward a door that was ajar and landed in a heap on the floor of the science laboratory. The poor elderly teacher, Miss Hare, was slap-bang in the middle of a delicate experiment involving magnets and ball bearings. When Alfie crashed through the door, she dropped her large box of ball bearings. It smashed to the floor, which within seconds was awash with hundreds and hundreds of tiny bouncing metal balls. As Alfie climbed to his feet, a huge number of them rolled under his shoes at speed. Soon it was like he was wearing a set of roller skates which had a crazed mind of their own. The boy started rocking and rolling all over the classroom, as if he were a very drunk person trying to dance.

The prim and proper Miss Hare shouted, "You, boy, come here!" She made a dash for him. However, the ball bearings spun under her shoes too. She started sliding around her classroom like an emu on ice. Unable to stop herself, Miss Hare tumbled through the air. The science teacher's legs were now where her arms had been. Worse than that, her knickers were where her head had been.

Miss Hare had flashed her knickers to the

entire class. The pupils, who had been expecting nothing more exciting that afternoon than seeing some ball bearings roll slowly toward a magnet, exploded with laughter. Now they had had a good look at their teacher's knickers.

And these were no ordinary knickers. Oh no. These knickers were rather large and rather frilly, almost Victoriany*.

The laughter turned to gasps as an outsize lady on an undersize moped knocked the door off its hinges as she exploded through it.

Winnie revved the engine until it roared. "Get on the back of my bike, boy!"

Just then Mr. Snood and his drama students caught up. They crowded around the door frame so they could watch the "impro" continue to unfold.

"No!" shouted Alfie. "Never!"

Made-up word* **ALERT

"Mmm, what did I tell you last term?" commented the drama teacher to his students. "Important rule of impro. Anybody...? No? In any impro always say 'yes'! Saying 'no' is an impro no-no."

Alfie made a dash to the left, and the bike lurched to the left. He made a dash to the right, and the bike lurched to the right.

Then he dived down on to his hands and knees to try to scuttle to the door under the rows of desks and stools.

By this time Miss Hare, now completely red-faced at the incident that would surely live in school legend forever as **"KNICKER-GATE,"** had righted herself. Smoothing down her pleated tweed skirt as if nothing had happened, she took off after Alfie too. The science teacher grabbed the back of his blazer, her hands gripping on to the cloth with all her might. Alfie jerked his body forward.

Miss Hare lost her balance and tumbled backward. Once again those knickers that seemed to have traveled through time now traveled through space as well.

This was **"KNICKERGATE II"** or **"KNICKERGATE: THE SEQUEL,"** as it would surely become known. Winnie skidded back over to the classroom door on her moped so she could block Alfie's way out.

"Give up, child!"

"No!"

"You can't go on running forever..."

"And you can't go on..." Alfie desperately searched for the right word. "...mopedding* forever!"

He never found it.

The boy had no way out. The door was

Made-up word* **ALERT

blocked by Snood and his herd of drama students. Jumping out of a window wasn't an option as it was three stories down. Alfie was trapped.

15

Bobsleighing Down the Stairs

Alfie wasn't going to go down without a struggle. He leaped on to the teacher's desk at the front of the class, landing beside a tray with some magnets on it. Next to it was another box full of ball bearings. In that instant, a daring plan flickered across the boy's mind.

First, he hurled the box to the floor, scattering the ball bearings.

Next, he grabbed the tray and held it to his chest.

Last, he launched himself onto the ball bearings, and shot across the classroom floor.

It was as if he were a one-man bobsleigh team. Alfie whizzed under the legs of Snood and shot straight out of the classroom door.

The ball bearings spilled down the corridor, and Alfie, still lying on the tray, found himself sliding at speed along it. Looking back, he saw Snood and his pupils with ball bearings trapped under their feet trying desperately to remain upright. As Snood was rolling over he called out, "Roll with the impro!"

The tray careered past classrooms before it reached the top of the huge central staircase.

Oh no! thought Alfie, as he closed his eyes.

The tray…

CLUNKCLUNKCLUNKED

…down the stairs, each step shaking his bones.

TUT-TUT-TUT.

Winnie's moped was gaining on him, with Hare, Snood, and their collective classes in pursuit. Just as the tray had reached a speed where it was impossible for Alfie to stop it, he spotted a figure at the bottom of the stairs. It was the headmaster, Mr. Grey, no doubt retreating to the safety of his office.

With every...

CLUNK CLUNK CLUNK

...the tray was gaining momentum at an alarming rate. As Alfie accelerated down the stairs, he quickly realized he was on a collision course with the headmaster. Nothing could stop the inevitable from happening.

Thwack!

The tray whacked into Mr. Grey's ankles.

The headmaster was hurled into the air. In

the smash, Alfie came clean off the tray, and ended up in a crumpled heap at the bottom of the stairs.

"Sorry, sir, I would love to stay around for you to give me a detention...," said Alfie as he hobbled up and helped Mr. Grey to his feet, "...but I really have to go."

With that, the boy burst out of the door that led outside into the playground. Just as the headmaster was about to call after him...

WALLOP!

...the poor man was thrown into the air by a large lady coming down the staircase at top speed on a moped. Mr. Grey landed with a...

THUMP!

...on his bony bottom. As he sat there, the headmaster could have been forgiven for thinking his ordeal was over. He was wrong. Very wrong. No sooner had he pulled himself back up than he landed with a...

THUD!

...as he became the victim of a stampede.

Once again Mr. Grey was trampled underfoot. This time by a number of his own teaching staff, and a growing horde of pupils who were giving chase. Because of all the commotion, they were streaming out of the classrooms. There was a boy on the loose! And he had to be stopped! They pursued Alfie out into the playground.

Next the dinner ladies joined in. They trundled out of the dining hall as fast as their chubby little legs would carry them, angrily brandishing their ladles. The caretaker stopped raking leaves in the car park and became part of the mob, waving his rake wildly in the air.

"Imaginative use of a prop!" commented Snood.

Even the ancient secretary, Miss Hedge, shuffled out on her Zimmer frame. "I'll get him!" she cried, hobbling along way behind the throng, traveling slower than the speed of treacle.

Leading the rabble was Winnie, racing after Alfie on her moped. "STOP THAT BOY!" she shouted, but the boy kept running.

Alfie ran and ran and ran. He was not naturally sporty, and had never run so fast in all his life. Disappointment set in that this moment wouldn't somehow count in the Olympics. Surely he was breaking a world sprint record?

Glancing back, Alfie saw there were now hundreds of people chasing after him.

It was one boy against an army, but he wasn't giving up yet.

Ahead of him he saw the huge iron gates that led out on to the main street.

Surely the whole school won't follow me out there? thought Alfie.

He was wrong.

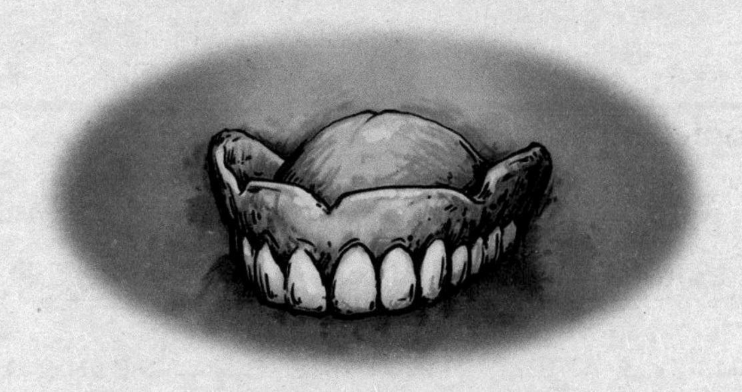

16

A Beckoning Hand

"STOP THAT BOY!" bellowed Winnie, as Alfie dashed past some mothers pushing their babies down the street. The women turned their prams around, and soon the infants were bouncing up and down as they too joined the chase. A lollipop lady, a homeless man, even a group of workmen who were meant to be digging up the road but as always were actually just drinking tea, reading newspapers, or wolf-whistling at attractive women all joined the hunt.

Winnie spotted PC Plank, who was idly patrolling up and down the road and somehow managing to miss everything that was going on. She bellowed at him:

"STOP HIM, OFFICER!"

At last the policeman realized that this was his moment. This was what all those years in Police Training College had been leading up to. Her Majesty the Queen was going to personally award him a medal for bravery. The octogenarian Scotch-egg thief was small fry. Now was the time. Time to save the day. Plank's time.

So he broke into a light jog.

"Oh, it's you! Come back here, boy!" he shouted ineffectually. After only a few paces of light jogging Plank was puffed out. Power walking also proved too much. Soon even walking was out of the question. Leaning on a wall to get his breath back, the policeman spluttered into his radio.

"Plank to base. I require urgent backup. Repeat. Urgent backup. Am knackered. Repeat. Knackered. And can you pick me up a bag of ready salted crisps on the way? Repeat. Ready salted crisps. Urgent. Over."

Alfie carried on running. He didn't know where to. He just had to run. Racing around the corner, Alfie saw a street with a rather sad-looking parade of shops ahead of him. Most of the shops had long since closed and been boarded up.

Sirens squealed.

Plank's backup from the police station had arrived. In an instant two police cars swerved into the middle of the road and screeched to a halt, blocking his way. The officers leaped out of their cars and took cover behind the bonnets. One of them spoke through a loud-hailer.

"Give yourself up, boy! You have nowhere to run to..."

"Did you pick me up some ready salted crisps?!" Plank radioed through to them.

"Negative!" came the crackled reply on Plank's radio. "No more ready salted left. We got you cheese and onion! Over."

"I don't like cheese and onion," replied Plank. "Repeat. Negative on the cheese and onion crisps. Over."

Alfie looked behind him. He couldn't go backward. He couldn't go forward. There was nowhere left to run to. Winnie smiled and smacked her lips. A smug grin surfaced on her face.

"You, boy, are going to the dentist!"

She had won. Or had she...?

Suddenly Alfie heard a creak. His eyes darted toward the parade of shops. A door was slowly opening, and a long thin hand emerged and beckoned him inside. It was his only chance of escape. Without hesitating he scurried toward it, crept through, and then slammed the door behind him. Outside he could hear the commotion of people rushing toward the door, before Winnie's voice announced, "No! It's OK! Leave him now!"

There was something deeply unnerving about all this. Why did they not follow him inside? It was all too easy.

As quickly as the hand had appeared, it had disappeared. Its owner was now nowhere to be seen. Directly ahead of Alfie was a narrow flight of steps. Tentatively he approached them. At the top of the stairs another door opened. Again the hand appeared, slowly beckoning him to follow.

Now he could see the long thin fingers more closely, they seemed almost too long to be human. A terrible fear descended upon Alfie, but try as he might to stop himself his body kept climbing the steps. One by one, until he reached the door at the top. Alfie's heart was beating faster now than when he was running. His mouth was as dry as a desert. Slowly he entered the room.

A circle of blazing white light shone toward him. Brighter and hotter than the sun. Blinking, Alfie could just about make out a figure. It was a woman. With hair the shape of a Mr. Whippy ice cream. The light behind her was so dazzling that he couldn't see any more than her outline.

"Hello, Alfie," came that familiar voice in its singsong tone. "I've been expecting you..."

17

Come to Mummy

Without Alfie even touching the handle, the door shut slowly and firmly behind him. There was the sound of a key being turned. Somehow he was locked in.

"How splendid! Two p.m. precisely! You are right on time for your appointment. Come on in..."

Miss Root's voice had a hypnotic quality to it. As much as Alfie knew in his mind he should run away, his legs propelled him forward. He was moving slowly and surely toward her.

"Come to Mummy...," she whispered.

As he drew closer, he could see the source of bright light was a vast Anglepoise lamp. Now Alfie was standing in her shadow he could make out Miss Root more clearly. Looking up at her, the first thing he noticed were her huge gleaming white teeth. As big as the ivory keys on a grand piano. Next he noticed her eyes. Those eyes. Those black eyes. Those eyes so black that it seemed if you gazed into them too deeply, you would see your own death.

Then Alfie could feel his body gliding over to the dentist's chair. It looked ancient, like an antique.

"Don't worry, young Alfie, Mummy promises to be gentle with you..."

As Alfie found himself sitting on the chair, it tilted back into position. He glanced down to one side. There was her trolley again, this time crowded with a staggering array of dental tools. Many were rusted, with old blackened wooden handles. Some had flecks of blood encrusted on them. They looked more like things you would find in a museum of medieval torture than a modern dental surgery.

There were ones with short spikes and ones with long spikes. There were chisels. Hammers. Pliers. One that looked like a giant corkscrew. Even a baby hacksaw. Stretched out at the end of the line, taking pride of place, was a huge and malevolent drill.

Not one of these tools looked designed to relieve pain. They all looked like they would cause it. In heart-stoppingly* eye-wateringly* bum-clenchingly* measure.

Alfie's eyes darted around the room. The surgery was quite bare. A dental certificate took

---

Made-up word* **ALERT
Made-up word* **ALERT
Made-up word* **ALERT

pride of place on the wall, but the paper and the writing looked like they could be hundreds of years old.

Pristine medicine cabinets lined the surgery, most holding tubes of Miss Root's highly toxic toothpaste. In the corner of the room was a long shiny gray metal cylinder, no doubt containing nitrous oxide or "laughing gas," often used by dentists on their patients to take away the pain. Curiously, on the dial was what looked like a speedometer. It read:

SLOW
MEDIUM
FAST
VERY FAST
REALLY TOO FAST
OH MY WORD MAKE THIS
THING STOP NOW

The surgery windows were all painted black, so no one could see in or out.

"Hhhhhhhhhhhh hiiiiiiiissssssssssss...!"

Alfie was startled, then looked down to see that a silky white cat had snaked into the surgery. It hissed in the boy's direction, its back arched and tail up, pink padded feet pitter-patting into the room.

"Oh, don't mind Fang...She's just being friendly. Now relax, child. Let Mummy take good care of you...," incanted the dentist. Miss Root pulled a lever somewhere behind the headrest of the reclining chair. In an instant, metal cuffs emerged, holding Alfie's hands and feet in place.

"Don't you worry, child. These are just for your own safety. So you don't lash out...!"

Smiling, Miss Root dressed her hands in latex

gloves. She took her time, enjoying the ritual of smoothing the glove over each long thin finger. Next, she picked up some notes from a bloodstained cardboard folder.

"Now, Alfie, I see your last visit to the dentist was six long years ago...Tut tut tut..."

Miss Root put the folder back down and pulled the lamp close to the boy's face. It was so hot it felt like fire.

"Open wide, there's a good boy..."

The dentist's eyes were now staring deep into Alfie's. As much as he wanted to cry out, he couldn't. Resistance was futile. Those black eyes of hers were spellbinding. It was as if they had him in a trance.

With his mouth dry with fear, the dentist's latex gloves squeaked as she traced her index fingers over the tops of his teeth. Now Alfie could feel Miss Root's cold breath on his face, as she leaned closer to peer into his mouth. "Tartar, decay, plaque, gum disease. Heavenly. Absolutely heavenly...!"

Alfie heard the ancient instruments *Clink* **clank** together as one was selected.

"Now Mummy's just going to check for any cavities," she continued.

Miss Root picked out a particularly evil-looking instrument. It was more like a spear than a dentist's implement, with a series of sharp prongs, each one wider than the next. It looked like it was designed to create intense pain as it entered the tooth, and even more coming out.

"Don't worry, Alfie, you won't feel a thing...," singsonged Miss Root.

She guided the tool inside his trembling mouth, before plunging it into a tooth.

"Mmm...Lots of lovely decay in this tooth... What a find you are!"

Slowly the dentist pulled the instrument out of the boy's tooth, twisting it sharply as she did so. Inside his head he screamed with pain, but no sound came out of his mouth.

Clink **clank**. The tool was put back on the trolley.

Clink **clank**. A new one was selected.

Now it was the turn of the pliers to assist in the torture, their metal jaws impossibly sharp and jagged.

"Now hold still, Alfie...," whispered Miss Root, as she steered the pliers slowly into his mouth. The jaws locked on to his tooth. "Mummy won't hurt you..."

She tugged the instrument sharply. Alfie could feel something coming away inside his mouth. Then, through a thick film of tears, he saw the dentist brandish a bloody tooth in front of his eyes...

"Look at it!" she urged. "To you, it's just a tooth. To me, it's like a diamond. Its very imperfections make it perfect. It's beautiful."

Then she called out to her white cat. "Fang...?"

The animal leaped up from the floor and landed on Alfie's stomach, her sharp claws digging into him. The cat began to lick the tooth clean of the blood that was now dripping down her mistress's wrist.

"Now relax, Alfie," said Miss Root in her jolly tone. "Mummy's only just begun...!"

18

Gurning Champion

Alfie must have passed out.

His eyes were closed.

Perhaps this was a dream.

He opened his eyes.

At first all he could see were patterns. Colors and shapes. After a few moments, Alfie realized he was staring at the ceiling. These colors and shapes were in fact sprays of blood. Some looked very fresh, still wet and glistening. Some looked brown and flaky, like they had dried there years before.

This was no dream.

Alfie realized he was still lying on the dentist's antique chair. He must have been lying there quite a while, and his back was hot and clammy with sweat. Behind him, somewhere out of view, he could hear that singsong voice again. This time it was counting...

"...eighteen, nineteen, twenty..."

What was she counting? With each number he heard something small and solid like a stone being dropped into a metal dish.

"Twenty-one!"

The final number was spoken with a particular flourish. Again there was a chinking sound of something hitting metal.

Twenty-one what? thought Alfie.

He could feel that there was something different about himself, but he couldn't quite work out what. He started with his toes. He wiggled them. From there he moved up his body.

ANKLES ✓
KNEES ✓
HANDS ✓
ELBOWS ✓
SHOULDERS ✓
NECK ✓

Then he moved his tongue around his mouth. Somehow it felt much larger now. Smooth too. Alfie traced his tongue into the furthest corners of his mouth. He could swear he could feel holes. Great big holes that seemed the size of caves.

It was then that Alfie realized.

He had no teeth.

The metal cuffs that had been holding his ankles and wrists had retracted back into the seat. The boy leaped up, and banged his head on the huge hot lamp that had been hovering over his mouth earlier. Swinging his legs round he jumped to the floor.

On the trolley sat a dirty old cracked mirror. He grabbed it and held it up to his face. Alfie was sure the dentist was behind him, but she was nowhere to be seen in the mirror's reflection.

Opening his mouth slowly, he could see only darkness inside. His gums were bare, and swollen. The only future for him now, he found himself thinking, was that of a gurning champion. (Gurning is the ancient art of pulling stupid faces. Champion gurners often have no teeth, even have them removed, to make their features easier to maneuver.)

Alfie moved his face in front of the mirror. In horror, he discovered he could now easily look like...

- A fish.
- A man who is sucking his own nose.

- An old lady who has swallowed a fly.
- A walnut.
- A puppet.
- A frog puckering up for a snog.

"Woken up now, have we...?" said Miss Root brightly. From a corner of the room, she turned to face him, her huge teeth glinting.

"WHAT HAVE YOU DONE WITH MY TEETH?" shouted Alfie. Well, that's what he tried to say. It actually came out as:

"WHA HA OOH DO IV MMM TE?"

"I'm sorry...?"

Alfie tried again.

"WHA A OOOOOH DOOO IVA MA TEE!"

"I'm terribly sorry, child, I didn't understand a word of that. Is something the matter...?"

"OV CAU SOMMON I VE MAA-AAA!" yelled the boy. "OOV TADEN OU AH OV MA TEE!"

"I still can't understand a single word you are saying! Would you mind writing it down here for Mummy…?"

The dentist passed him a pile of appointment cards and a pen. He wrote furiously on one.

WHAT YOU DONE WITH MY TEETH?

it read. The letters were large and pointed and angry.

Miss Root studied it for a while.

"Mmm, I think what you are trying to ask Mummy is, 'What HAVE you done with my teeth?'"

Alfie was fuming now. He was sure Miss Root knew full well what he meant. This was just another of her ways to slowly torture him.

"WHA HHAA OOH

DOOOO IV MA TEEEE EEEEEEEEE!!!!!"

"Please don't use that tone with Mummy..."

Alfie was staring the lady right in the eyes now. She held his gaze. And glared back. The pupils in her eyes shone black. On second look, they were blacker than coal. Blacker than oil. Blacker than night. Blacker than the blackest black.

In short, they were black.

"...so what have I done with your teeth...?"

Alfie nodded his head up and down, each nod more enraged than the last. Fang was sat on top of Miss Root's trolley, and now she started hissing in short sharp bursts as if she was laughing at him.

"Hiss...hiss...hiss..."

"Not to worry, child, Mummy's kept them

safe for you. All the little beauties are in here..."

With that she carefully lifted a little metal dish up to Alfie's ear and rattled it gently. The noise made her face light up with joy.

Alfie peered inside. There were his teeth. Every last one. All sadly piled on top of each other. Admittedly, they didn't look at all healthy. The years of missing dental appointments had taken their toll. They were all stained brown from too many sweets and fizzy drinks. However, did the dentist really need to remove every single one...?

Alfie finally realized what she had been counting. His teeth.

(A twelve-year-old boy is meant to have around twenty-four teeth, but Alfie had less than that. Mr. Erstwhile, the old dentist who died mysteriously, took one out all those years ago. And after that one or two had fallen out.)

"WHA YO GOOIN DO?"

"Would you mind awfully writing it down again for Mummy...?"

Miss Root gestured once again toward the pad of appointment slips.

Once more Alfie scribbled furiously.

WHAT ARE YOU GOING TO DO?

he wrote. The dentist studied the piece of paper for a moment. "Is that a 'G' or a 'Y'?"

Alfie growled at her.

Miss Root read the sentence out loud. "'What are you going to do?' Mummy's got it right, hasn't she...?"

Alfie nodded, and Miss Root furrowed her brow in thought. "Well, normally at the end of any appointment I would come out with the normal dentist's spiel...come and see me in another six months, don't forget to floss, think about investing in an electric toothbrush, blah blah blah... But there's no need for you to do any of that, Alfie. You see, you don't have any teeth anymore, and they are never ever growing back."

With that the dentist guided the poor toothless boy out of the room, before adding cheerily, "Good day!"

19

Frozen Paper

Alfie was lost. He knew where he was, but he didn't know where he should go.

Home? He didn't want Dad to see him like this. It would upset him too much.

School? This could be a brutal enough place at the best of times. The boy with no teeth? That's what he would become. Forever. Having a brace or big front teeth that made you look like a bunny rabbit was bad enough.

Alfie realized there was only one place to go...

DING!

The bell at the top of the door of Raj's newsagent's rang as the boy entered the shop. It served to alert the shopkeeper that a customer was either coming or going. Also it woke Raj up. He was a big, soft, marshmallow of a man, and although he loved selling sweets, he loved eating them even more. After the rush of sugar following a mid-afternoon scoffing session, he would often fall asleep at his counter.

Indeed, when Alfie entered this particular afternoon, Raj was snoring away with a gobstopper still in his mouth. A slick of the newsagent's spit was spreading over the newspapers. Raj woke up with a start, spat out his sweet and exclaimed:

"Ah, young Alfred! My favorite customer!"

His voice was as bright and colorful as the confectionery he sold.

Alfie always looked forward to seeing Raj. The newsagent knew how poor he and his dad were, and being a kindhearted man he would often give Alfie a treat to take home. A melted ice lolly, a chocolate bar that had been slightly nibbled by a rodent, or a bag of jelly babies that Raj had accidentally sat on so all the tiny tots were now flattened. Raj wasn't a wealthy man, and couldn't afford to give anything more. But to Alfie and his father they were like gifts sent from heaven, and the difference between going to bed hungry or not.

Entering Raj's shop today, the boy couldn't even force a smile.

"You are very quiet this afternoon, young man," mused the shopkeeper. Squinting his eyes, he took a better look at his favorite customer. In truth, Raj had a lot of "favorite" customers, but calling them all that made them feel special. "There is something very different about you today..."

Raj came out from behind his counter to give the boy a closer inspection.

"You've had a perm! No no no..." That thought was dismissed as soon as it had been thinked*.

"Mmm, you've had one of those far too orangey spray tans! No no no..."

Raj lowered his head so he was staring the boy right in the face. Alfie opened his mouth, to reveal the full extent of his toothlessnessness*.

The newsagent peered inside. "I've got it!" exclaimed Raj. "I've got it!"

Alfie nodded his head in encouragement. It couldn't be more obvious now.

"You've had your teeth whitened!"

The boy rolled his eyes.

"Oh, no no no. That's not right, is it?"

Made-up word* **ALERT

Alfie shook his head.

"You've had all your teeth removed!" Raj then repeated what he had just said a hundred times louder, double-checking if it could really be true.

"YOU'VE HAD ALL YOUR TEETH REMOVED?!"

The man was so flabbergasted he needed to sit down, and he sank onto a large box of crisps. Unfortunately he was far too heavy for it, and within seconds his weight had flattened the box completely and he was lying on the floor. The bags of crisps had all exploded and tiny flakes of crisp now showered the shop.

"Oh dear," said Raj, as he tried to heave his generously proportioned bum off the ground. "Remind me to knock a penny off the price of those crisps," he added as he fumbled to his feet.

"But why, boy? Why? Why have you had all your teeth removed?"

Alfie had given up trying to talk for now, and mimed the international sign language for "pen and paper" by pretending to write.

"The bill? No! No! Pen and paper!" guessed Raj. "I'm good at charades!" The newsagent started rushing around his shop trying to find some paper and a pen. His shop was infamous in the town for being incredibly messy. It was never easy to find what you wanted, not even for the owner.

"I think there are some Post-it Notes in the freezer cabinet, just under the choc-ices..."

He slid open the glass roof, and reached inside.

"I don't remember why I put them in there," he muttered. "At least they won't have gone off..."

Next Raj scurried over to the other side of his store. "A pen!" he exclaimed. "I think I put one in a sherbet Dip Dab a while back. I ate the licorice stick, so I popped a black felt tip in. Not as tasty as the licorice, I'll grant you, but still an effective way of enjoying the sherbet."

After a short while Raj identified the correct Dip Dab and pulled out the pen. It was coated in the fizzy white powder.

"Sherbet?" asked Raj, as he offered Alfie the pen. "No?"

Alfie shook his head, so Raj licked it clean before handing it to him. "Slight taste of ink..." he mused, "...otherwise fine. So tell me, young sir. What on earth happened?"

A hundred frozen Post-it Notes later, Raj had been told the whole story. By this time, Alfie was crying hard. What had happened to him had finally sunk in. Raj gave the boy a much-needed hug. The newsagent was big and fat and squishy. He was good at hugs.

"You poor thing," said Raj, as Alfie's tears soaked the man's bright orange shirt.

"I am so angry with that Miss Root! First she goes into the local schools and gives out free sweets. Taking away all my customers. And now this..."

Poor Alfie couldn't stop crying. Raj patted him gently, and the boy sniffed.

"You can blow your nose on that *Hello!* magazine. Now wait there, I have an idea..."

20

Joke-Shop Gnashers

"Well…?" asked Raj. "How do they fit?"

Raj had gone upstairs to his flat above the shop, and brought down his late wife's false teeth in a glass of water for the boy to try for size. They looked a bit like those joke-shop gnashers that you wind up and watch clatter across the table. To Alfie's surprise though, they fitted rather well. They weren't perfect. The dentures had been specially made for a middle-aged woman. They rubbed here and there, but they were infinitely better than having no teeth at all.

"Are you sure you don't mind me borrowing them?" asked Alfie, delighted to discover that he could at last talk again.

"No, no, no. It's what dear Mrs. Raj would have wanted."

"Thank you so much."

"Might you have any use for her glass eye, rubber hand, or either of her wooden legs?"

Alfie was quite taken aback. After all, he had never met the late Mrs. Raj. Not that there seemed that much of her to meet.

"Very kind of you," he replied, "but no..."

"Not kind at all. Just part of the service. That's why people should always support the smaller local shops. You wouldn't get that from a supermarket!"

"True!" replied Alfie, though he wasn't sure

many customers at a supermarket would need a loan of some secondhand false teeth.

"Though I would advise you not to go anywhere near a toffee," warned the newsagent. "I remember these dentures came clean out of my late wife's mouth when she bit into an out-of-date Toffo I gave her on our silver wedding anniversary."

"I will remember that...," said Alfie. "So, how can we stop Root? My teeth were bad, but not that bad. There was no way on earth she needed to take out ALL of them. She's evil!"

"Now I come to think of it," pondered the newsagent, "there have been strange goings-on in this town ever since she arrived."

"Like children putting their teeth under their pillows and finding something nasty in the morning!"

"Exactly!" exclaimed Raj. "How did you know?"

"It happened to my girl friend Gabz…"

"Your girlfriend?! Ooh…," cooed Raj.

"No, no!" exclaimed Alfie. "She isn't my girlfriend. Gabz is just a friend who's a girl."

"Your friendgirl*?"

Alfie thought it was easier to simply agree. "Yes, I suppose so. Gabz has drawn a map charting exactly where and when the teeth were snatched…"

"The whole thing is sickening. When I was little, or at least smaller than I am now, and I lost a tooth, I would put it under my pillow, and when I woke up I would find a coin in its place. From the tooth fairy."

"Well, your mum or dad must have left it there," replied Alfie.

Raj looked mightily confused. "But they

Made-up word* **ALERT *(Any letters of complaint to be addressed to Raj.)*

told me it was the tooth fairy…"

Alfie sighed. He was very nearly a teenager. To still believe in tooth fairies was just plain silly. As far as he was concerned, the thought that a tiny winged figure in a tutu and holding a wand came into your room at night to leave money under your pillow was preposterous. However, he didn't want to hurt the newsagent's feelings.

"Well, I think sometimes it might be the tooth fairies, but when they are busy, mums and dads help out," replied Alfie. "Go on, Raj…"

"Well, quite a few of my younger customers woke up this morning to find not a coin, but all sorts of nasties under their pillow."

"Like what?" asked Alfie.

"Oh, there were… cockroaches…"

"Anything else?"

"Oh, let me think. Dead worms, a live rat, a toad that had been flattened by a mallet and dried out in the sun until it was crispy..."

The boy brought his hand up to his mouth. He felt sick at the thought of all these horrors. Still, his ghoulish curiosity got the better of him, and he wanted to hear more.

"Was that all?" he inquired.

"No." Raj took a deep breath. "Are you sure you want to know the most gruesomest* one?"

"Yes and no," replied Alfie. "But mainly yes..."

Raj took a deep breath before telling him.

"An old man's toenail!"

"No!" cried Alfie.

"Yes. Nobody knows who it belonged to. All big and thick and dirty it was, with all this dried pus around the edge..."

"STOP!" shouted Alfie.

"You said you wanted me to tell you!" protested Raj.

"Yes! But I didn't know it was going to be

Made-up word* **ALERT

that disgusting." Alfie thought for a moment. "And none of these children saw a thing?"

The newsagent shook his head. "Not one. Nobody saw a thing. It's a mystery. And how could one person possibly get around to all those children in one night?"

Alfie pulled himself up on to the shop's counter and sat there next to the till. "But there must be some kind of connection with Miss Root. There must be! I swear she is evil," he said. "We need to catch her red-handed! Lay some sort of trap..."

Alfie fell silent and stared into space. Raj looked at him.

"A trap?" asked the newsagent.

"I am thinking, Raj..."

"Oh, my apologies." Raj mooched around awkwardly for a few moments. "Would a mint help focus your mind?"

"I've got it!" exclaimed Alfie. His eyes were shining, and he leaped off the counter in excitement.

"Got what?"

"A plan! How we can catch the tooth snatcher!"

"Great, my boy! That's brilliant. How can I help?"

Alfie looked right into Raj's eyes for a moment. He knew what he was about to say was not going to go down at all well. "It's just a very small thing..."

"Yes...?" said the newsagent.

"I need to borrow one of your teeth..."

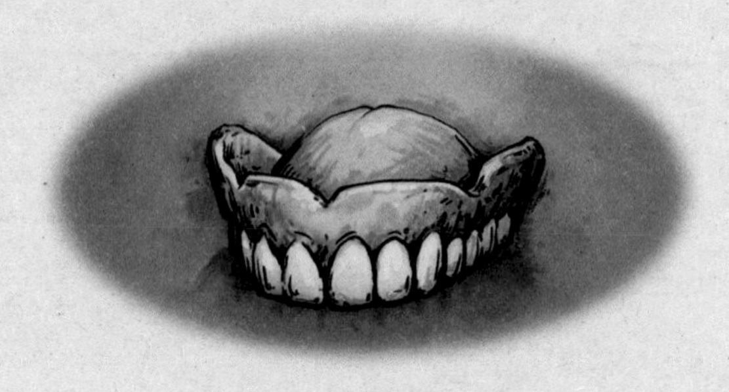

21

Flying Tooth

"One of MY teeth...?" protested Raj.

"Yes," replied Alfie firmly. "I would offer one of my mine, but I don't have any left."

Raj was not convinced. "But why do you need one of my teeth?"

Alfie paced up and down the penny chew aisle to compose his thoughts.

"OK. This much we know...Someone or something is taking the children of the town's teeth from under their pillows and leaving something despicable behind, right?"

"Yes," agreed the newsagent.

"So tonight I am going to leave a tooth under my pillow when I go to bed, then pretend to be asleep."

"Coffee Revels will keep you awake! I can separate them out from the other more palatable flavors."

"Good plan. Then I will lay in bed with half an eye open, to catch sight of whoever or whatever..."—the boy gulped in fear—"...is responsible for this evil..."

Raj nodded, and then looked away so as not to catch Alfie's eye. The newsagent pretended to straighten some packets of pastilles. "Well, best of luck, young man. I won't keep you any longer. Good day!"

Alfie watched the newsagent for a while. Eventually he said, "Raj...?"

"Yes?"

"Aren't you forgetting something...?"

"No, I don't think so," replied Raj a little too quickly. "I don't want to keep you, so..."

"Your tooth..."

Raj looked more than a little panicked, and slowly approached Alfie.

"I would love to lend you one of my teeth; well, I suppose it would be more of a gift," said the shopkeeper. "But..."

"But...?" prompted the boy.

"I am scared taking it out is going to hurt."

Alfie's brain had been processing different ways they could remove one of Raj's teeth. There seemed to be a sliding scale of pain:

MINIMUM PAIN:

- Try and tempt it out with the promise of a highly paid advert for toothpaste.

- Eat sugar cubes day and night for fifty years and wait for it to fall out.

BEARABLE PAIN:

- Wiggle it for years until it finally comes loose.
- Bite into an out-of-date toffee, and then remove toffee and tooth in one go.

MAXIMUM PAIN:

- Tie a piece of string from the tooth to the door and then slam the door.
- Crunch into a mint humbug without sucking it first.

OH MY GOODNESS:

- Poke it out with a pencil.
- Attach the tooth to a dog using a piece of cord and then call the dog's name

from the other side of the room.

MAKE IT STOP NOW:

- Ask a professional snooker player to pot it out with his cue.
- Get a big fat boy to flick a conker at it.

Tying the tooth to a door and slamming it seemed by far the best option. Not least because it would be over in a second. What's more, Raj sold string in his shop. It was of course kept just underneath the body-building magazines.

Reluctantly, Raj went along with the plan.

First, Alfie tied one end of the string to the newsagent's tooth.

Next, he carefully measured out the distance from Raj, who he had stand behind his counter, to the open door.

Then, with just a tiny bit of slack, he tied the other end of the string to the open door's handle.

"All right, Raj, stay very still, and I will count down from three. On one I will slam the door…," pronounced Alfie.

He slowly began the countdown.

"Three…two…"

Before he could say one, a little old lady came in through the open door, and pushed it shut behind her.

screamed Raj, as his tooth shot across the shop hitting the poor old dear on her head.

"You said one! You said you would slam the door on one!" the shopkeeper protested.

Alfie rushed over to the old lady, who was rubbing her forehead and looking utterly dazed and confused.

"Are you all right?" he asked.

"Yes, I think so, dear. I only came in for a scratchcard and a bag of bonbons..."

"Ah, Mrs. Morrissey, my favorite customer..." Raj gathered himself, and approached the lady with the items. "Here we are! And don't worry, madam, there is no extra charge for being hit in the head by my flying tooth..."

The befuddled old lady reached into her purse and handed him the money, before the newsagent gently guided her out of his shop.

Meanwhile, Alfie gathered up the string and

smiled at discovering Raj's tooth was still at the end of it. He briefly examined its chips and stains before popping it in his pocket. "Thanks, Raj. This will be the bait..."

"Well, best of luck, young Alfred. And I expect you to come here to the shop first thing tomorrow morning to tell me if you saw anything in the night."

"I will."

Raj rushed back to his counter. Quickly he sorted through a dozen or so packs of Revels, putting all the coffee ones in one bag. Then he carefully resealed them all with a glue stick.

"Nearly forgot! Here's a bag of coffee-only Revels to keep you awake. There might be the odd raisin one in there as they are a very similar shape..."

The newsagent placed the bag in the boy's hand, and held it tight for a moment. He looked straight into Alfie's eyes and whispered, "For goodness' sake, boy, be careful..."

"I will, Raj."

DING!

The boy opened the door to leave.

"One last thing...," whispered Raj.

"Yes?"

"Don't tell anyone I have tampered with these bags of Revels..."

22

A Gigantic Trifle

"So how did it all go at the dentist, son?" rasped Dad, his breathing painfully shallow. "Did you have to have a filling?"

Alfie's father was sitting in his wheelchair in the living room as his son came in through the front door. It was around four o'clock, the normal time that Alfie returned home from school, so his dad didn't yet have a reason to suspect anything.

"Oh, it was fine, thanks, Dad!" called Alfie,

as cheerily as he could. The false teeth rattled a little in his mouth.

Alfie could see his dad's health was worsening by the day. The man was becoming weaker and weaker, like he was shrinking into his wheelchair. Alfie feared that if he told his dad the truth, he would get angry. Really angry. Dad would want to speed over to the surgery instantly, and have it out with this dentist. If the boy's father started shouting or even raised his voice, his breathing would become shallower and shallower. He might even collapse again. Alfie couldn't let it happen.

Awkwardly the boy shuffled into the room. When Alfie came home from school he always gave his dad a big hug, but today he loitered by the door. He didn't want his father to be able to inspect his teeth. Well, the late Mrs. Raj's teeth. Her false teeth, that is.

"No hug today, pup?" Dad appealed to him. This break in the habit made Alfie's father suspicious.

"I was just going to put the tea on..."

"The tea can wait. I've been sitting at home alone all day looking forward to our hug. And I want a big bear hug, please. The biggest, widest, huggiest* hug you can give!"

Carefully Alfie closed his mouth and sucked the late Mrs. Raj's false teeth into place over his gums. Next, he paced across to his father's side of the room. Leaning over the wheelchair, he put his arms around Dad, and the man held him tight.

"Ah, that's better. How I love my little pup..."

Telling lies to his dad made Alfie feel distinctly uneasy. It was a horrible sensation, which found its way down to the pit of his tummy. In shame

---

Made-up word* **ALERT

and embarrassment, Alfie was soon trying to disentangle himself from the hug.

Now, parents always know when something is wrong with their child. They can sense it. Dad was no different.

"Are you sure there is nothing the matter?" he asked, looking his son right in the eye.

"No. I mean, yes...," spluttered Alfie, attempting to avoid his dad's gaze. "Yes, I am sure. There is nothing the matter. The dentist went fine."

"Let me have a look at your teeth..."

Reluctantly, Alfie opened his mouth, and flashed the briefest of smiles before closing it again. "See? Like new."

"Well, they do look better...," said Dad.

"I'll pop the kettle on."

With that, Alfie scurried out of the living room and into the relative safety of the kitchen.

Alfie placed the blackened tin kettle onto the

little camping stove in the center of the room, and lit the gas. The gas from the mains had been disconnected years ago. Bills in red ink had replaced bills in black ink until one day there were no more bills at all. And no more gas. With Dad unable to work for so long, they just didn't have enough money to pay for everything.

As Alfie waited for the water to boil, he reached into his pocket, to check that the tooth Raj had so generously donated to his daring plan was still there. With a sigh of relief, he felt that indeed it was. Now all he had to do was wait for nightfall.

And of course, try and stay awake…

The gas in the tiny stove spluttered to its end just as the kettle whistled. The water had boiled, but now they were completely out of fuel. This was the last cup of tea they were going to have for quite a while.

Alfie reentered the living room with two

cups of tea but no biscuits, because yesterday afternoon their social worker had eaten them all.

"Thank you, son," said Dad.

All seemed well, until...

KNOCK KNOCK KNOCK.

There was somebody at the door. Alfie's heart skipped a beat. The knocks were loud and insistent. Was it Mr. Grey the headmaster, come to tell Dad his son had been expelled? Was it PC Plank, come to arrest him after the mayhem he had caused in town today? Or Mr. Snood the drama teacher, still hoping to carry on the impro?

"Sounds like Winnie...," said Dad.

No! thought Alfie. *I can't let her in, she'll tell him everything!*

"I'll ask her to come back later," he said.

"No, son," said Dad firmly. "Let her in. She's

so thoughtful, she's probably just stopping by to see how you are feeling after your trip to the dentist's..."

KNOCK KNOCK KNOCK KNOCK KNOCK...

"Let her in!" said Dad again.

Alfie rushed to the door. He had to try and stop her, stall her, anything. Through the mottled glass, her multicolored clothing made her look like a gigantic trifle. Alfie took a deep breath, and turned the handle.

"Ah! Hello, Alfred. We meet again!"

"I'm sorry, Winnie, this isn't a good time...," he whispered.

"It's OK, I won't stay long," she said. "Just a very quick chat to Mr. Griffit and I'll be on my way."

With that she bustled past Alfie. In her job

as a social worker, Winnie was well-practiced in people not wanting her around.

- Busybody.
- Meddler.
- Pest.
- Stirrer.
- Do-gooder.
- Nuisance.
- Troublemaker.
- Botherer.
- Bossy boots.
- Biscuit thief.

Winnie had been called them all, and worse. Much worse. As a result, she had developed a very thick skin, and was well-used to people slamming the door in her face. At quite a pace she scuttled along the corridor; Alfie could do nothing more than follow in her wake.

"Please, please, please don't tell my dad about what happened today..." His whisper was becoming louder now. It was almost like a shouted whisper, if such a thing were possible, but Winnie seemed determined to ignore his plea.

"Good afternoon, Mr. Griffit!" she exclaimed theatrically as she entered the living room. Dad's face grimaced a little. Even he found her a tiny bit annoying, her voice a few notches too loud...

Dad squinted as he tried to take in what the social worker was wearing today. This time Winnie had outdone herself. Her collective clothes, bangles, and makeup were sporting more shades of color than would be found in even the widest set of coloring pencils.

"Ah! Tea! Thanking you kindly!" She picked

up Alfie's cup, had a loud slurp…

“SSSSSSSSSSSLLLLLLLLLL
LLLLLLLLLLLLUUU
UUUUUUUUU
UUUURRRRR
RRPPPPPPPP
PPPP!!!!!!”

…followed by an even louder sigh, then dropped down on to the sofa with all her weight. Winnie hit it with such force that a huge cloud of dust burst from the cushions into the air.

“Have a seat, Winnie…,” ventured Alfie's father, a little too late.

“Dad, please, don't listen to her. I can explain…,” said the boy, panicking in the doorway.

“Oh, I can't wait to hear this!” pronounced Winnie.

"Alfie has told me virtually nothing about his trip to the dentist," Dad said. "Perhaps, Winnie, you can tell me what happened."

"Dad, please believe me," pleaded the boy. "I was going to tell you..."

"Oh, Mr. Griffit, it's quite a story. Quite a story...," said the lady.

Alfie was sure Winnie was about to drop him headfirst into an enormous vat labeled "trouble."

"Let me get comfortable," she said, plumping up the cushions behind her and stretching out her legs. "This is going to take some time..."

23

Jet-Powered Bottom

"Before I begin," continued Winnie, lounging on the sofa like Cleopatra, Queen of the Nile, "I would like one of your delicious biscuits?"

Since Dad's illness had confined him to a wheelchair, Alfie had become responsible for all the food shopping. He knew that the bungalow was a certified biscuit-free zone.

"You ate the last one yesterday," said Alfie. "Remember?"

"Cake?" she trilled, with a hopeful and

teasing lilt in her voice. "A nice slice of cake?" Winnie looked like the kind of woman who, when offered a piece of cake, would leave the slice and take the rest...

"No," replied the boy. He didn't need to check. They never had cake. Not even on birthdays.

"Oh dear, oh dear, oh dear...," mused the lady. "Chocolate?"

"We don't have any," replied Alfie.

"Nothing chocolaty in the house?" persisted Winnie.

"No."

"Nothing chocolate covered or chocolate flavored?"

"No."

"Chocolate chipped coated swirled layered sprayed encrusted sprinkled blended melted or dipped...?"

Alfie took a breath before replying. Winnie

was being so annoying it was hard not to shout. "There is nothing in any way chocolaty in the house…"

There was a long pause.

"Infused?" With that, Winnie was back in the game.

"No!"

"Nothing infused with chocolate…?"

"No!!"

"Nothing with even a hint or a whiff or a trace or a suggestion of chocolate…?"

"NO!!!"

"Something that's not meant to have chocolate in but might have chocolate in by accident…?"

Both Dad and Alfie looked flummoxed by this.

"Like what?" asked Dad, who had been watching this contest as if it were a tennis match.

"Yes, what?!" implored the boy.

The lady looked deep in thought for a moment. "Well, that could really be anything that is labeled chocolate-free?"

"**No!!!**" barked the boy. "We don't have anything chocolaty, chocolate flavored, chocolate infused or chocolate chocolated*!"

"All right!" huffed Winnie. "I only asked..."

With that she slurped her tea...

"SSSSSSSSSLLLLUU UUUUURRRR PPPPPP!!!!"

...and sighed again.

"AAAAAHHHHHHHH!!!!!!"

Alfie perched on the edge of the armchair, next to Dad, and folded his arms. Now he was ready to accept his fate. As he leaned back a

Made-up word* **ALERT

little the packet of all-coffee Revels that Raj had given him fell out of his trouser pocket and onto the floor. In a heartbeat, Winnie's eyes were on them, like a killer whale that's just seen an overweight seal plop off an iceberg and into the sea.

"Well then, young Alfred, what on earth could that be?" she teased. She knew perfectly well it was a bag of chocolate-coated confectionery.

"Nothing," Alfie replied quickly.

"It's not nothing, son," chimed in Dad, unhelpfully. "It looks to me like a packet of chocolates..."

Winnie stared at the boy.

"Oh, *these*, yes, sorry. When you said chocolate covered, coated or infused I didn't think that included Revels."

There was a hush, before Winnie whispered, "I think you know full well that Revels are a chocolate-coated confectionery."

"Offer the nice lady one...," prompted Dad.

Alfie needed those sweets. If he ate one every half an hour, those chocolate-covered coffee creams would keep him from falling asleep. Without those much-needed shots of caffeine, what chance would Alfie have of catching whoever was responsible for leaving the unspeakable horrors under children's pillows?

Reluctantly he picked up the packet, and sloped over to Winnie.

"Thank you, young man. Well, we got there in the end! Now, which flavor Revel shall I have...Mmm...I like them all apart from the coffee ones..."

"No one likes the coffee ones...," agreed Dad.

Good luck, thought Alfie. If Raj had sorted

them properly like he said, every single one was coffee.

"I can't have coffee anyway," continued Winnie, "it goes right through me..."

Dad and son shared a look that said simply, "too much information." Neither wanted to imagine what this lady looked like glued to the toilet.

Greedily, Winnie ripped open the bag and helped herself. She picked out the first Revel and popped it in her mouth. She chewed for a moment, before her face contorted as the sour taste of coffee slipped down her throat.

"No! It's coffee...," she moaned. "The first one too! What rotten luck!"

Now it was Alfie's turn to smirk. He had to bury his head in his shirt to hide his ever-widening smile.

"Let me have a different one to take the taste away...," she said.

So Winnie helped herself to another Revel. Again her face soured.

"Coffee again! No! I need a different one!"

Had Raj managed to sort the Revels correctly? Or had he left the odd rogue raisin Revel in? Alfie was praying he hadn't.

Winnie selected another. "Ah, this one must be toffee! My favorite of all the Revels…"

Carefully she began inspecting the tiny chocolate.

"Or orange cream…? No, no, no, this is definitely toffee. The good Lord is finally smiling upon me!"

After rolling it, sniffing it, and even licking it, she finally put the Revel in her mouth. It melted on her tongue and as soon as the chocolate coating had dissolved, Winnie's face once again contorted in complete and utter revulsion. It was as if a deadly poisonous jellyfish had swum straight into her mouth.

"C O F F E E ! ! ! NNNNNNOOooooooooOO!!!!!"

she whined.

Then she took another, and another and another. Each one gobbled in hope to take the taste of the last one away. Each one just making it worse! Soon the whole packet had been well and truly demolished. And Winnie had a belly full of coffee. She sat there on the sofa, with chocolate around her mouth and an expression of pure misery on her face.

"Every single blasted one was coffee!" she protested.

"Oh dear…," uttered Alfie, trying his hardest not to burst out laughing. "How could that have happened?"

Dad looked very surprised. "What are the chances of that?!" he asked. "It must be a million to one!"

His son tried to look as innocent as possible, which somehow made him look extremely guilty.

But now was the calm before the storm. Then, out of the silence came a sound. A long, low rumbling sound. It was like a storm was breaking in some far-off mythical land. Dad and Alfie looked at each other, and then turned their gazes to Winnie. The poor lady looked down to her round tummy. It was rumbling and grumbling and expanding at an alarming rate. It was as if it were a balloon that was so full of air it was about to pop.

"I TOLD YOU COFFEE GOES RIGHT THROUGH ME!" exclaimed the woman. "MY BOTTOM IS ABOUT TO EXPLODE!"

"Well," mused Alfie, looking more than a little smug, "I suppose your story will have to wait for another day..."

"Yes! Yes! I have to go!" exclaimed Winnie. "Now! Right now!" With that, Winnie went to stand up. As she straightened, her bottom burped. Loudly and violently. "In fact, now is too late." There was another bottom burp, even louder and violenter* than the first. "Oh, dear, excuse me!"

The lady was deeply embarrassed to have lost control of her bottom so completely. She squatted down a little as she scuttled out of the room sideways like a crab. Winnie was desperately hoping to contain the wind, but with each step out of the room her bum let rip a thunderous blast of air.

Alfie found this so hilarious he had tears in his eyes now. Dad, who was not meant to find this funny as he was an adult, had his hand over his mouth to stop himself from sniggering too. As they heard the door slam behind her, the pair finally erupted with laughter, hooting and

---

Made-up word* **ALERT

honking like sea lions. Dad laughed so much that he slid out of his wheelchair and plopped on to the floor. They rolled around for a while on the carpet cuddling and laughing.

Eventually Alfie shuffled over on his knees to the window to watch Winnie zoom off. The moped seemed to be going a hundred times faster than usual. Perhaps her bottom, with the coffee-scented gas whooshing out of it, was functioning like a powerful jet engine?

With the social worker gone, Alfie was out of trouble. For now. But the boy was about to step into a world more dangerous than he could ever imagine…

24

The Darkest Hour

The plan was under way…

It was still early, but Alfie was in his pajamas and ready for bed. He placed Raj's tooth under his pillow. Tonight he didn't need any prompting from Dad that it was his bedtime. As soon as darkness fell, Alfie went straight to his room. No one knew what time this someone or something would strike and snatch the tooth. It just had to be dark. And it was dark already. Real, winter dark.

There was now one big problem with Alfie's

plan though. How on earth was he going to stay awake all night? Winnie had scoffed every last coffee Revel. There were plenty of other methods for staying awake, but none of them seemed foolproof:

- Put matchsticks between your eyelids to keep them open.
- Drink gallons of water and then don't go for a pee before bed.
- Slap yourself hard in the face every minute.
- Leave the window wide open. It will become so cold you will shiver and icicles will grow from your nose.
- Picture your least favorite teacher, and then try and think of ten things you like about them. It's impossible!
- Give yourself the mother of all rug burns. The pain will keep you awake.
- Get out of bed every five minutes and do a

rhythmic gymnastics routine. Ball or ribbon will do.

- Lie in bed in an awfully uncomfortable position.

Alfie climbed into bed, and blew out the flame on the candle he was holding. As he lay there, he realized he didn't need any of those tricks to stop him from falling asleep. He had never felt so wide awake in his entire life. At first the night seemed still and quiet. But soon every little sound, even the tiniest creak or rustle, filled his mind with fear...

IT COULD BE THEM.
IT COULD BE THEM.
IT COULD BE THEM.

Shadows began to dance on the walls. Were these nothing more than the silhouettes of trees illuminated by the headlights of passing cars? Or perhaps they were something more sinister?

IT COULD BE THEM.
IT COULD BE THEM.
IT.
COULD.
BE.
THEM.

Alfie kept sliding his hand under the pillow to check the tooth was still there. It was.

Who or what was going to come into his room? And how would they try and snatch the tooth? Lying there in the dark, his imagination started to run wild. Soon it was hard for Alfie to distinguish between what was real and what was in his mind. Was he lying in bed awake? Or was he actually asleep and simply dreaming he was awake?

Hours passed. Or was it minutes? It was impossible to tell. Now outside Alfie's window there wasn't a sound. Not a bird singing. Not a plane in the sky. Not even a distant car. This truly was the darkest hour.

He slid his hand under his pillow once more. The tooth was still exactly where he had left it.

Just then Alfie heard something rustling in the bushes outside. It could be a bird or a squirrel or even a rat. But no, the sound was too loud; this was something bigger.

There was silence for a moment.

Then as quick as lightning a shadow loomed outside the window, blocking out the yellow glow from the streetlamps entirely. It was horrifying. Suddenly facing the terror alone seemed like a catastrophic mistake. Alfie was frightened. Dead frightened.

Next he heard the window slide open. Then

the worn and bedraggled curtains were drawn aside, as the figure climbed into his room. Alfie wanted to cry out, but his mouth was dry with fear and he couldn't make a sound. Soon the shape was plodding slowly toward him. Alfie's plan was to pretend to be sleeping, let the tooth be stolen, and sneak a look at the perpetrator as they left. However, this plan was unraveling, and fast. Alfie was in such a panic now there was no way he could keep still. His whole body was trembling in terror.

It was fight or flight.

With the figure closing in on him, there was nowhere to run. To fight was the only option. Alfie leaped out of bed. He charged toward the figure, making wild circles in the air with his fists as he cried…

"AAAAAHHHHHHHHH!!!!!!!!!"

25

Under the Pillow

"AAAAAAAAAAAAA AAAHHHHHHHH!!!!!!" shouted the figure, before adding, "Please, please, please don't hurt me!"

It was the unmistakeable voice of Raj.

Alfie lit the candle by his bed with a match, and brought it closer to the shadowy shape. It was the unmistakable face of Raj.

The panic over, Alfie swallowed hard, and croaked, "Raj! What on earth are you doing here?!"

"You frightened me!" exclaimed the newsagent.

"You frightened me more!" replied the boy.

"Well, I think you frightened me more."

"No. You actually frightened me more."

"No no no no no! You definitely one hundred percent frightened me more!" protested Raj. "And no returns."

There was little point arguing with the man. The newsagent was well-known for being frightened easily. Local gossip had it he once ran out of his shop screaming after he swore he saw one of his two-pence jelly snakes moving.

"All right, all right," conceded Alfie. "But I thought you were, you know, the tooth snatcher..."

"I'm not," replied Raj. "My name is Raj. And I am your newsagent."

"Yes yes yes! I know who you are!" said the

boy, exasperated now. "What are you doing here…?"

At that moment, what seemed like a huge gust of freezing cold air came in through the window. It blew the candle out.

"It's dark in here!" whimpered Raj.

"It's OK, just let me find my matches…"

Alfie groped by his bedside table (which was really just an upturned milk crate) and lit the candle. Now his bedroom felt decidedly chilly, so he moved over to the window and closed it. Feeling more than a little spooked, he locked it too.

"Well, I was lying in my bed above the shop and I couldn't help worrying about you, all alone waiting for this…" Raj struggled to find the right word. Finally he settled on, "…thing."

"Well, that's kind of you, Raj, but honestly I was fine," lied Alfie. "It must be the middle of the night now, but there has been absolutely no sign of anything."

"And my tooth is still under your pillow?"

"Oh yes," said Alfie, moving over to the bed. "I put it just here. Look..."

But when the boy lifted the pillow the tooth wasn't there.

Something else was.

Something horribly horrible.

Something dreadfully dreadful.

An eyeball.

The long silky nerve at the back was still attached. It was flailing about as if it were a tail, making the eyeball twitch and wriggle on the mattress like a tadpole on dry land.

"AAAAAAAAAAA
AAAHHHHHHHH!!!!!!!"

screamed Raj.

Alfie, who as we know thought of himself as being a tiny bit braver than the newsagent, screamed too:

"AAAAAAAA AAAAAAAAAAHH HHHHHHH!!!!!!!"

The boy's scream was even louder.

"It's an eyeball!" screamed Raj.

"I know!" said Alfie.

"But it's an actual eyeball...!"

"Yes, but let's all try and stay calm," said the boy. "This is a clue..."

Alfie slowly and steadily brought the candle down to examine the eyeball. It was unusually large. It was the size of a ping-pong ball. The eyeball had to be from a large animal. Or perhaps a giant.

Just then the eyeball turned and looked straight at him.

"AAAAAAAAAAAAAAAAAAAAAHHHHHHHHHHHHHH!!!!!!!!!!"
screamed Alfie.

"AAAAAAAAAAAAAAAAHHHHHHHHHH!!!!!!!"
screamed Raj.

"It looked at me!" spluttered the boy. "It looked at me straight in the eye..."

THUMP

THUMP

THUMP

Someone was banging on the wall.

Raj screamed again, and tried to leap into Alfie's arms.

"That's my dad in the next room..."

"Oh, sorry," said the newsagent, trying to calm himself. His nerves were shot to pieces tonight. "I always leaped into my mother's arms whenever I saw a mouse..."

"Well, you are too heavy..."

"I know. Mother told me that when I tried to do it last week."

Alfie looked at the newsagent, utterly incredulous.

THUMP

THUMP

THUMP

Dad was banging on the wall again.

"Son? Son? Are you all right?" he coughed and spluttered from the next room.

"Just coming, Dad..."

Alfie rushed out of his room and down the corridor to his father's bedroom, the petrified newsagent trailing close behind.

"Raj...?" asked Dad, really quite bemused.

"Ah, hello, Mr. Griffith...," said Raj brightly, pretending that being in the man's bungalow in the dead of night was perfectly normal.

"Look, if it's about the newspaper bill, I was meaning to...," began Dad.

Raj smiled. "My friend, the newspaper bill has been long forgotten."

"So what are you doing here?" asked Dad.

Raj looked over to Alfie. Dad followed his gaze. Suddenly all eyes (well, apart from the one in the room next door) were staring at him.

"Well...?" said Dad. "I think it's about time you told me the truth, my lad!"

"My lad" was something Dad only called Alfie when he had done something wrong. Alfie knew that. He took a deep breath. It was finally time to tell his father the whole story...

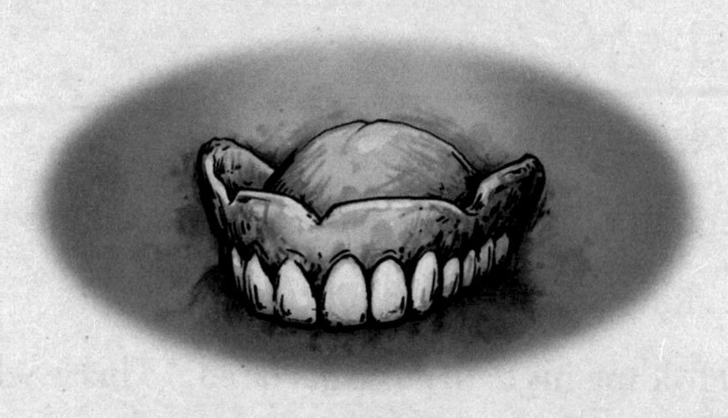

26

Thick Brown Slime

Fantastical tales were Dad's speciality. However, this one he struggled to believe. With some prompting from Raj, Alfie told his dad the whole story...the dentist's visit to the school... the special "MUMMY's toothpaste" that burned through stone...the tooth snatching happening every night...being chased by the entire town... and finally having all his teeth taken out. Dad's disbelief turned to anger when Alfie took out the false teeth and held them up to the candlelight.

"When I get my hands on that dentist...," shouted Dad, before he was plunged into a coughing and spluttering fit.

Holding his dad, Alfie declared, "This is why I didn't want to tell you! I didn't want to upset you..."

Alfie's father looked deep into his son's eyes.

"I am more upset you didn't tell me, son... We're a team, aren't we? You and me?"

Alfie nodded; he was afraid his voice would crack with emotion if he spoke.

"You're my pup. My little pup...," continued Dad. "And I would do anything for my little pup...I would die for you, if I had to..."

A tear welled in Alfie's eye. Even Raj was blubbing, and had a big old blow of his nose on his sleeve.

Soon the pair had helped Dad into his chair, and he wheeled himself into the next room to inspect the final and most gruesome piece of the puzzle...

The eyeball.

Thankfully by now it had stopped twitching and wriggling. However, it had left a trail of thick brown slime all over the sheet where it had traveled. The three faces peered in to inspect it by candlelight.

"The strangest thing is," began Alfie, "I swear I was awake all night. So how could the tooth have been switched with this without me knowing?"

Dad thought long and hard, before replying.

"You must have nodded off at some point, son."

"No," said the boy. Alfie was absolutely sure. "I didn't. And I kept checking under the pillow all night. In fact, I checked just before Raj came in, and it was still there..."

"You shut the window behind me…," added Raj.

"Just after that freezing gust of wind…," Alfie thought aloud.

"Yes," agreed Raj. He inspected the window. "And look, it's still locked…"

Then all three fell deadly silent. Out of the gloom Dad whispered, "Then whoever or whatever did this must still be in the bungalow…"

None of them moved a muscle.

"In fact, it could still be in this room…," he whispered.

Three sets of eyes darted around in the dark. If this was true, where could it be hiding? The room was cramped. There were only a couple of pieces of furniture. It was not ideal for a game of hide-and-seek.

With his eyes, Dad indicated the old wooden

wardrobe standing in the corner of the room. Alfie started to tiptoe over to it, holding the candle. His body weight landed on a loose floorboard and it creaked loudly. Dad put his finger up to his lips, and Alfie rebalanced his weight quickly. With two more silent steps he had his hand on the wardrobe door. Dad nodded his head gently, to indicate that his son should open it. The suspense was too much for Raj, who was already cowering behind Dad's wheelchair, and had now closed his eyes.

The boy pulled the handles sharply. Something flew toward him…

His anorak. The sleeve must have been caught in the door.

After taking a breath, Alfie pushed his few items of clothing aside, but there was nothing evil lurking in the cupboard. Aside from an old unwashed football sock, that is. It had been lying there so long it now had yellow and green mold growing on it.

Throughout, Raj's eyes remained tightly shut, his face grimacing in fear. Dad tugged at the newsagent's arm and he startled like a wild horse, leaping into the air as his whole body contorted in fright.

"AAAGGGAAAGGGH!"

he neighed.

"Sssshhhh!" shushed Dad, and with his eyes he pointed to the bed. Raj pointed to himself and assumed an expression which said, "Me?"

Dad nodded, with an expression which said, "Yes! You!"

The newsagent shook his head. He put his hands together in prayer, begging Dad for it not to have to be him.

Alfie rolled his eyes. He stepped forward and gently pushed the cowardly newsagent aside. Pulling up the sheet, Alfie bent down with the candle in his hand to look underneath the bed. It was dark under there, and even with the candlelight he squinted as he tried to make anything out in the shadows. Like most boys, Alfie never bothered to clean under his bed. So there were long-forgotten pieces of Lego and a pair of dirty old underpants loitering there. All looked ghostly gray, smothered in a thick covering of dust. Alfie sighed. Again there seemed to be nothing evil hiding there…

Then. Under the bed. Out of the darkness. Two eyes opened. And fixed the boy with a deathly black stare.

"AAAAAAAAAAAA AAAHHHHHHHH!!!!!!!" cried Alfie.

The owner of those eyes then blew Alfie's candle out. Now the room was all but pitch black. A shadowy figure rose from under the bed. Without stopping to unlock the window, it flew straight through it with a deafening roar. It moved at such speed that shards of smashed glass exploded out of the room.

Alfie hurried to the window frame. He needed to catch a glimpse of whoever or whatever had been hiding under his bed. The boy looked out into the dark night. Something rocketed down the road and then soared up and up and up into the sky. Higher and higher it rose until it flew through the clouds. Soon all that was left behind was a trail of black smoke.

Alfie closed his eyes. Surely they were deceiving him?

Opening his eyes again, he saw that the trail was still there.

This was no nightmare.

This was real.

Alfie had no option. He had to believe.

27

A Case of the Willies

PC Plank didn't look best pleased to be dragged out of his warm comfy bed in the middle of the night. The policeman still had his stripy pajamas on, but had put on his police cap to try and give himself some sense of authority. With a torch, he examined the smashed window in Alfie's bedroom. He traced the beam of the torch around the frame, before shining it on the shards of glass on the floor. Finally the policeman announced, "This window has been smashed."

Alfie rolled his eyes. "Yes, we've established that..."

Plank shone the torch right into the boy's eyes. "Less of your lip, sunshine. You are lucky I don't arrest you. Littering, wasting police time, not stopping when requested by an officer of the law."

Dad was becoming increasingly frustrated with the policeman. His breathing was growing more and more uneven. "Listen, Constable, something very serious happened here tonight. Someone..."

"Or something...," chimed in the newsagent.

"Thank you, Raj...," spluttered Dad, "...or something, came into my son's bedroom in the middle of the night, and left that revolting... thing...under his pillow."

PC Plank shone his torch on the eyeball, still glistening on the bed.

"Hmm...," he hmmmed*. "Just the one eyeball, was it?"

Made-up word* **ALERT

"What?!" replied Alfie, utterly bemused by the line of questioning.

"Well, they normally come in pairs, don't they?" Plank defended himself. "Two would be worse, but I suppose one is still bad..."

"Yes, Plank. An eyeball under your pillow is bad! Very bad...," replied Dad, before breaking into a terrible coughing fit.

"Seeing it gave me an awful case of the willies!" added Raj.

"Gabz and I told you this was happening," said Alfie. "Now you've seen it with your own eyes. I am no detective but I know that eyeball is a really important piece of evidence. Shouldn't you be taking it away and examining it for fingerprints or DNA?"

"Yes, yes...," replied PC Plank. "But no, no..."

"No?" said Alfie.

"You see, I've run out of my special evidence

bags. Me mum used the last one tonight for me sandwiches, in case I got peckish..."

"Oh, for goodness' sake!" said Dad.

The policeman produced the sandwiches from his pajama pocket. "Jam...," he announced, before taking a bite of one. "Mum makes a very nice jam sandwich, takes the crusts off for me, an' all."

Large saliva-sodden crumbs dropped from his mouth onto the eyeball.

"Erm...," said Plank as he munched away. "Have you got any clingfilm in the house I can wrap the eyeball in?"

"No!" replied the boy angrily.

"Hmmm...," the policeman hmmed* again. "Let me think...," said Plank as he finished his sandwich. "I've got it. Can you post it to me?"

"What?" said Dad between coughs, unable to believe quite how stupid this man was.

Made-up word* **ALERT

"Yes! Pop it in a Jiffy bag, slap a second-class stamp on it, I should get it by Monday..."

"That will be too late!" cried Alfie. "How many times do you need to be told?"

"Normally about three or four at least to really get through...," replied the policeman without irony.

"Look! Every night kids are putting their teeth under their pillows and waking up to something horrible like this!" pleaded the boy. "You have to do something!"

"ALL RIGHT!" protested PC Plank. "A first-class stamp!"

It was a relief when the useless policeman finally left. Raj went home soon after. He insisted on calling himself a taxi for the one-minute ride back to his flat above the shop. He was far too spooked to walk home alone.

Dad and Alfie cuddled up in bed together. Not only had the boy been scared out of his wits, his father had too. But even with his dad's arm around him, Alfie couldn't sleep a wink that night.

His mind was racing, replaying the events in his head over and over again. Was that freezing gust of wind really the tooth snatcher entering his room? And those eyes under the bed. There was no denying it. Alfie had seen those eyes before. Those black eyes. Now he had to confront their owner.

Soon dawn was breaking, the sunlight burning through the holes in the curtains. As Dad snored, Alfie gently lifted his father's heavy arm off him and tiptoed silently back to his room. Everything in there was covered in a silvery frost. With the window smashed, the room had become freezing cold. As quickly as he could, Alfie dressed and popped his false teeth back in. Looking out of the window frame as he zipped up his coat, there was no sound. Not even the birds were singing yet. It was still very early, and the boy knew that this was his chance. Last night had been all too much for his dad's health. Raj's nerves made him a liability. As for Gabz, this was all now way too dangerous for him to want to involve the little girl.

He was going to have to face this monster alone.

28

Out of the Fog

After closing the front door of the bungalow as gently as possible so his father wouldn't hear him leave, Alfie ran through the empty streets. His destination: the dentist's surgery.

This winter morning a thick mist hung in the air. Where possible, Alfie kept close to the walls and hid in the shadows; there was the chance someone or something could be following him. Just down the road a little from the surgery stood a knotted old tree.

Trudging through the soggy fallen leaves at its roots, Alfie hid behind the trunk. From there he fixed his eyes on the dentist's doorway.

The boy squinted to see if he could make out the lettering on the door. *Miss Root, MDW*, it read. *Dental Practitioner*.

As the boy pondered what "MDW" might stand for, above his head he heard what sounded like the hum of a jet engine. His eyes darted upward. Out of the fog, Alfie saw a figure emerging, flying at speed through the air high above the buildings, astride what looked like some kind of gas cylinder. Something else was perched on the back too. After circling overhead a few times, the duo began their descent. Even though the town was cloaked in fog, as they came down, the boy had a clearer and clearer view. Soon Alfie could see who it was without a shadow of a doubt.

It was Miss Root, the dentist.

Riding her laughing gas cylinder.

The something else perched on the back was Fang. Before long they reached the ground.

The dentist turned a dial on the front of the cylinder, and the contraption came to a halt at the surgery door. She hopped off with the ease that someone might get off a bicycle.

That's how she managed to zoom all over town every night! thought Alfie.

Despite having just flown through the air, Miss Root looked remarkably composed. Not only were her clothes immaculate, but not a hair was out of place on her head. Alfie ducked back behind the tree as the dentist stole a quick glance over her shoulder to ensure that no one was watching. Then she disappeared inside, her faithful white cat following close behind. She was carrying the cylinder under one arm, and a shiny metal tin under the other. It rattled as she walked. It must be full of children's teeth!

Alfie stood openmouthed in shock. She is a witch! he thought.

Miss Root might not wear black, or a pointy hat, or have a broomstick exactly, but she was a witch all right.

OWNS CAT ✓
FLIES AROUND AT NIGHT ✓
EVIL ✓✓✓

Gabz was right after all—witches were alive and well. Miss Root was walking proof. Well, flying proof. And now they were practicing dentistry. That's what the MDW must have stood for, a Master's degree in Dentistry and Witchistry*.

As soon as the door to the surgery had

Made-up word* **ALERT

closed behind Miss Root, the streets began to hum with people and traffic. Then from behind the tree Alfie spotted a little girl with a mass of dreadlocks approaching the surgery door. It was Gabz. True to what she had told Alfie in the playground yesterday, she was going to confront Miss Root herself. However, Gabz didn't know the full extent of the evil that lurked behind that door. She didn't know Miss Root had taken out every single one of his teeth. What's more, she hadn't witnessed the horror that Alfie had last night. Before he could shout out, Gabz had pressed the dentist's bell. In an instant the door buzzed open. Alfie had to warn his little friend. And fast.

He leaped out from behind the tree. But just as he was about to shout the girl's name, someone grabbed him by the back of his coat and lifted him high into the air…

29

Asleep on the Toilet

"I've been looking all over town for you, Alfred!" said Winnie. The social worker was holding the boy by the back of his coat. The toes of Alfie's shoes just scraped the ground.

"Put me down!" said Alfie angrily.

"Your poor father is worried sick about you!" The big lady placed him back down on the ground, but kept a firm hand on his shoulder. "I'm taking you straight home!"

"No, no, no, I can't go home..." Alfie felt guilty that he had run out without telling Dad where he was going. But it was an emergency.

Winnie sighed wearily. "Listen, young man," she began. "I am not in the best of moods this morning. After your little trick with the coffee Revels I had to sleep on the toilet!"

Alfie attempted to dismiss the image of that as soon as it took shape in his head. However, the more he tried not to visualize his social worker asleep on the lavatory, the more vivid the image became.

"Look! I have to get into the dentist's surgery!" pleaded Alfie.

"No, no, no!" scoffed Winnie. "First I am going to take you home. Then we have a little appointment with your headmaster. I am going to try and persuade him not to expel you..."

"I don't care if he expels me or not! I have to

get in there now!" shouted Alfie, pointing at the dentist's door.

Winnie's eyes narrowed. Try as she might, she couldn't understand this boy at all. "Yesterday the whole town had to chase you all the way there, now you can't wait to get in...?"

"I have to warn this girl friend of mine, well she's not my girlfriend, she's a girl who's a friend..."

"It's OK if she is your girlfriend...," mused Winnie.

"She's not."

"Sounds like she is," replied the lady, with a big grin on her face.

"She's not," repeated the boy firmly.

"No," said Winnie. "But just to say, it really doesn't matter if she is your girlfriend."

Alfie was becoming mightily frustrated now.

"Well, she's definitely one hundred percent

not my girlfriend! And no returns!"

The social worker fell silent for a moment, before continuing, "So this girl, who's a friend of yours, but definitely not your girlfriend, where is she?"

"Gabz. She's just gone into the dentist's surgery! She called me a scaredy cat for not wanting to go, but I have to warn her about the dentist..."

Winnie shook her head wearily. "That Miss Root seems like such a nice lady. What on earth do you have to warn Gabz about?"

"That the dentist is really..."

"Yes?"

Alfie knew it to be true, but still felt silly saying it. Finally he plucked up the courage to finish his sentence: "...a witch!"

The social worker looked at Alfie for a long while. Then a smile crept across her face before she burst into hysterical laughter.

"Ha ha! A witch, you say! Ha ha ha ha ha!"

"Yes," replied Alfie firmly.

"Ha ha ha!" Winnie was still laughing. "A witch? That's the nuttiest thing I have ever heard!"

"Well, it's true!" he exclaimed. "She flies around on this cylinder of laughing gas, that's her broomstick…"

"Ha ha ha!" laughed Winnie. "Next you'll be telling me she has a black cat!"

"White, actually. But it's really evil," replied Alfie.

"Ha ha ha!" The lady was wiping away a happy tear from her eye now. "Miss Root has become a respected member of the local community. And from what I have heard is an excellent dentist…"

Alfie looked right into Winnie's eyes.

"Really? Then why on earth would she do this to me..."

With that he took out his false teeth and showed the social worker exactly what Miss Root had done to him. Winnie gasped and brought a hand up to her mouth in shock.

"Oh no!" she whispered. "Miss Root did that to you?"

Alfie put his teeth back in before answering. "Yes. And right now my friend is up there in her surgery..."

Winnie looked up at the blacked-out windows. At that moment they heard the whine of a drill and then a blood-curdling scream from inside the surgery.

"Nooooo!" cried Winnie. "Come on, Alfred, there's no time to lose!"

30

Kneel Down Before Me

Winnie grabbed Alfie's hand, and together they raced up the street toward the surgery. The social worker was a big lady. Being a big lady, when she charged toward the door and slammed her shoulder into it, it started to buckle. After two attempts she beckoned to Alfie to jump onto her back to add a little more ballast.

This worked rather well, and on the fourth attempt the door smashed out of its frame and crashed to the floor. Together they flew up the stairs and burst into the surgery.

Gabz's wrists and ankles were fastened to the dentist's chair just as Alfie's had been. Miss Root loomed over the little girl, wielding a huge drill. Like all her dental tools, the drill looked more like an instrument of medieval torture. It wasn't electric. Instead, her hand circled wildly to make the thick drill bit on the end rotate. It was going so fast, it let out a high-pitched scream as it spun. It was so gigantic it looked like it was more suited to digging a hole in the road than in someone's tooth.

"Get away from her!" shouted Winnie.

Despite the drama, Alfie couldn't help but smile. Finally he and his social worker were a team.

"What is the meaning of this?" proclaimed Miss Root.

"I said get away from her," repeated the social worker.

The dentist pointed the drill toward Winnie and Alfie.

"Step back...," she growled.

"Let Gabz go!" said Alfie.

"Or what...?"

"Or I will write a very strongly worded letter to the British Dental Association...," replied Winnie.

"Help!" screamed Gabz, her entire body trembling with fear. "Root said she's going to take out every single one of my teeth!"

"Yes, I am...," sneered Miss Root.

With that she smiled, baring those too-white-to-be-real teeth of hers. She slowly raised her hand, and pulled those teeth out of her mouth. They were false all along. Lifting the veneers away, she revealed the true horror underneath.

A set of hideous fangs.

Each one sharper, more jagged, bloodier than

the next. They were so gruesome, they would not have looked out of place on a Tyrannosaurus rex.

"And none of you can stop me," the dentist continued. "You must kneel down before me. For I am the Tooth Witch!"

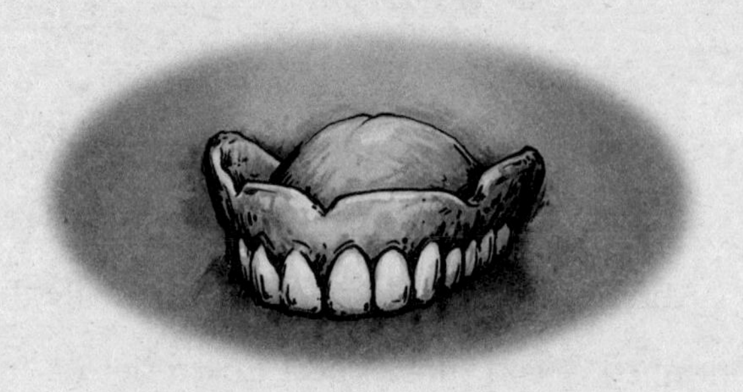

31

Swinging a Cat

Stepping out from behind Winnie, Alfie circled round the back of the Tooth Witch. Now the demonic one was wielding the drill this way and that to keep them both from coming close. From the cabinet behind him, he grabbed a tube of "MUMMY's" toothpaste. Fang leaped up onto the counter and launched herself at him, landing on his head. But the cat couldn't stop him squirting the paste straight at the witch's face. Most of it missed and just singed her hair, but as a few flecks of the toxic goo dropped into her black, black eyes, she fell to her knees in pain.

The drill fell out of her hand, and swirled around on the floor like a snake in the throes of death.

Winnie hurried over to the chair, and started trying to force open the metal clasps that bound Gabz to it. As she did so, Fang leaped from Alfie's head to Winnie's, the cat's thick white fur now obscuring the woman's face completely. One by one Fang's razor sharp claws came out, and the evil beast started digging them deep into Winnie's neck until they drew blood.

"HHHHHHH IIIIIIIIIIIISSSSSSSSSSSS SSSSSS!!!!!!!!" hissed the creature.

"Aaah!" screamed the social worker. "And I am allergic to cats!"

Thinking fast, Alfie grabbed hold of the beast's hard and bony tail, and with all his strength yanked the cat off his social worker.

Alfie had often wondered where the phrase "the room wasn't big enough to swing a cat in" originated. Now as he found himself swinging a cat by her tail in a small room, her head skimming the chair, the cupboards, even the walls, Alfie's understanding of the phrase grew.

After swinging Fang round and round, the most natural next step seemed to be to let her go.

Which is exactly what Alfie did.

Fang flew through the air, hissing wildly. The beast shot across the room, and landed with a *smash* on the witch's trolley.

All the deadly dental instruments scattered across the room to the floor.

"Nice one!" said Gabz.

"Thanks," said Alfie.

With Winnie nursing her wounds, and the witch still rubbing her eyes clear of the last of the toothpaste, Alfie frantically started trying to find the lever to open the metal clasps.

"You were right," he said breathlessly. "She is a witch!"

"DUH!" replied Gabz. "You don't say!"

The sarcastic tone took Alfie by surprise. "All right! Do you want me to rescue you or not?" he asked.

"Erm, yes, please...," said Gabz, adding a hopeful little smile. "That one there!"

"Oh yes, of course," said Alfie. Hastily he reached for the lever behind the headrest, and yanked on it hard. In an instant, the restraints retracted, and Gabz's wrists and ankles were freed. Like a knight in shining armor, Alfie tried to scoop Gabz into his arms but she was having none of it.

"I can manage, thank you!" said Gabz

dismissively. She was a tomboy at heart, and hated this new role she was being cast in as the damsel in distress. She swung her legs round and jumped down on to the floor.

"Let's go!" said Winnie.

Behind them, rubbing her eyes clear of the last of the toothpaste, the Tooth Witch slowly rose to her feet. Groping behind her with one hand she grabbed one of the ancient tools still left on the trolley. This one had a long sharp spiked hook at the end of it. With her other hand, the witch reached out and grabbed Gabz, pulling her violently toward her, and held the weapon up to the little girl's throat as she whispered...

"One step forward and your girlfriend dies."

Winnie and Alfie stood as still and quiet as statues. But the boy couldn't help himself and broke the silence.

"Just for the record, she is not my girlfriend..."

"Yeah!" scoffed Gabz, the hook almost piercing her skin. "As if I would go out with him!"

"Well, I would never ever in a million years go out with her...," agreed Alfie, a little hurt by quite how sure the girl sounded.

"I wouldn't go out with you if you were the last boy on earth!" replied Gabz.

"This is not the time!" shouted the witch. With that, she pulled the girl by her hair and backed over to the silver gas cylinder in the corner of the room. The witch climbed astride it, and placed the kicking and screaming Gabz in front of her. Then the witch leaned back, and turned the nozzle on the end of the cylinder. Just in time, Fang hopped up behind her and it shot off like a rocket. The three of them crashed through the blacked-out window. Alfie ran over to see them zoom off up into the sunless sky. A trail of smoke spilled out behind them.

"Quick, Winnie!" shouted Alfie. "We have to save Gabz!"

The pair raced downstairs, and leaped on to the social worker's moped. Alfie kept his eyes focused upward, directing Winnie after the trail of smoke. They sped through the town, traveling cross-country when necessary, taking shortcuts through back gardens, down alleyways, even through a supermarket. Poor Mrs. Morrissey had only popped in for a tin of spaghetti hoops. But as the moped roared past, she leaped out of the way, and fell headfirst into the ice-cream section. Within moments, an absent-minded shelf stacker had stickered her as being on "Special Offer."

"Sorry, Mrs. M!" shouted Winnie, before

exiting through the five items or less queue to save time. "I'll be round tomorrow afternoon as usual with the Meals on Wheels!"

As they sped out into the car park, the social worker pulled back on the throttle hard.

"Hold on tight...," she yelled, as the pair picked up the trail of black smoke once more. But now it looked like it had come to a stop somewhere just over the brow of the next hill. As they reached the top, Winnie brought the moped to a halt for a moment.

"Look," shouted Alfie over the hum of the engine, "the witch has taken Gabz into the old coal mine..."

"Oh no," said Winnie. "There's no way down..."

32

The Lower Depths

For many years coal mining in the town had been extinct. The mine itself had been boarded up. It stood there, ugly and unloved, in an ocean of its own slurry. To keep trespassers out, a huge metal fence encircled the mine. The fence was topped with a crown of barbed wire. Signs screaming *BEWARE! KEEP OUT!* and *DANGER!* were everywhere.

Alfie knew where there was a little hole in the fence. The older kids at school would often talk about it. Strange as it might seem, the old deserted mine held a fascination for many of the local youngsters. At the very least, it was somewhere for them to go of an evening to drink and smoke and snog, away from the prying eyes of grown-ups.

The hole in the fence was child-size, not big-lady-size, so Alfie thought it safest for Winnie to try and crawl through first. However, as soon as she tried to squeeze through, her clothes became caught on the metal edges of the wire.

"Help me, boy! I'm stuck!" she shrieked.

Alfie surveyed the scene. The social worker did not look at her most dignified.

"What do you want me to do?" he asked.

"Push!" she implored.

Alfie took in her position. All he could now see of his social worker were her more than ample buttocks.

"Where?" he asked innocently.

"My booty!"

Reluctantly he placed his hands on Winnie's abundant bum.

"PUSH!" she cried.

Using all his weight, Alfie pushed the woman's bottom, his feet slipping and sliding on the wet mud just outside the wire fence. Nothing. He took a deep breath and made another huge effort. It was a bit like pushing a car. But eventually Winnie passed through the hole.

Unfortunately her clothes did not.

The multicolored jacket, top and leggings remained hanging on the ends of the cut wire. It took a few moments for Winnie to realize she was now only in her underwear. "It's suddenly become rather chilly...," she muttered to herself at first, as she struggled to her feet. Finally, she looked down and saw that she was standing there in her bra and knickers. The bra was quite the biggest Alfie had ever seen. It looked like it could comfortably hold two footballs, and was bright orange. The knickers, that might have doubled as a child's play tent, were a shocking shade of pink. "Oh my!" Winnie cried. The poor lady looked dreadfully embarrassed.

As fast as he could, Alfie untangled Winnie's clothes from the fence. To respect her modesty, he turned his head away as he passed the now-torn garments through the hole.

"Oh, thank you, young Alfred," said Winnie, as she snatched them from him. Alfie didn't turn his head back until all the grunting and groaning as she struggled to put the dress back on had stopped. The social worker gave a deep sigh of relief, before telling Alfie, "Not a word of that to anyone, please!"

"Of course not, Winnie!" said Alfie, not sure he would quite be able to keep it secret forever.

"I wasn't wearing matching underwear today!" she exclaimed. "Oh, the shame of it!"

From where they stood, the pair could just see how the now dispersing trail of smoke ended exactly at the entrance to the mine. At the opening rested a huge metal cage, which itself housed a giant lift. In its long-lost days as a working mine, the lift would have taken Alfie's dad and all the other miners deep underground. Hundreds of meters down, in the dark tunnels, they would do their arduous work. Once upon a time, coal was the country's main source of energy. So for hours upon hours the miners would work, dig and chisel and drill, to bring chunks of the mineral to the surface. That was how Dad developed the terrible problem with his breathing. Over the years, all that dust from drilling the coal had become embedded in his lungs.

"The witch must have taken Gabz straight down there," said Alfie, as they raced across the rubble to the mine entrance. "My dad told me there is only one way down—in the lift. We have to go after them…"

Winnie held on to Alfie's hand to steady herself. It wasn't easy running on such loose ground in wedges. "Alfred, you're not going nowhere…"

"What?" answered Alfie. He hadn't come all this way for nothing.

"An old deserted mine!" Winnie exclaimed. "No, no, no. It's far too dangerous. And as your social worker I have a duty of care…"

Alfie couldn't hide his frustration as they finally reached the huge metal cage that housed the lift. "But if we don't go after the Tooth Witch now, who knows what she will do to Gabz?"

He traced his hand over the old controls that were caked in a decade of grime, searching for a button that might bring the lift up to the surface.

"Come away from there, boy!" shouted Winnie. "This instant!"

Like most kids being told not to do something, Alfie pretended not to hear. Eventually he found the large green button which must call the lift. Jamming his finger on to it, he pressed and pressed again, but the lift didn't make a sound. The power must have been cut off when the mine closed all those years before.

"See!" said Winnie. "There is no way down. Now the best thing we can do is wait here while I call the police for help…" She fumbled in her lime green handbag for her phone.

"That PC Plank is useless!" said Alfie. "We need to rescue Gabz now!"

Using all his might, he slammed ajar the huge rusty metal door that opened on to the lift shaft. He peered down into the blackness. For all he could see, it could go down for miles. Alfie picked up a small discarded piece of coal, and dropped it. In his head he counted how many seconds until he heard the thud of it hitting the bottom.

One, two, three, four, five, six, seven, eight, nine, ten, eleven…

It must be hundreds of meters down.

"Come away from the edge, boy!" shouted Winnie, pulling him back sharply by his hand. Alfie shook her away, and took several paces back from the shaft.

"Oh, thank goodness…," said Winnie with a relieved sigh. Little did she know that Alfie was actually taking a run-up. As the social worker was busy tapping a number into her phone, Alfie ripped out the insides of his trouser pockets and put them over his hands to use as makeshift gloves.

"It's ringing…," announced Winnie, as she

held the phone to her ear.

Just then Alfie sprinted forward as fast as he could. He took a running jump at the thick metal lift cable that was suspended from the top to the bottom of the shaft. It was greasier than he had anticipated. At first Alfie panicked, he couldn't get a grip, he started sliding down it nearly as fast as if he were falling. For a moment, he thought his short life might be over.

"Aaaaaaahhhhhh!!!!!!!!" cried Alfie.

"Nooooooooooooo!!!!!!!" cried Winnie.

As swiftly as he could, Alfie wrapped his legs around the cable and squeezed tight. Thankfully this slowed him to a stop. Using his hands, little by little he lowered himself into the mine.

"Come back!" yelled Winnie. Her voice echoed deep into the mine shaft.

It was too late. Alfie had disappeared into the dark depths below.

33

A Cathedral of Teeth

Above him, Alfie could see the square of daylight at the top of the shaft becoming smaller and smaller and smaller. As he slid further and further down, it eventually became nothing more than a tiny speck, no larger than a star in the sky. Now he was hundreds of meters underground. The muscles in his arms were tiring fast. There was no way he would ever be able to pull himself all the way back up. The only way was down. Eventually his feet touched something below him, though it was so dark for the life of him Alfie couldn't see what it was. It was blacker than black at the bottom of the mine shaft. **This is how dark it was...**

Despite it being pitch-black, Alfie guessed that his feet must have touched down on the top of the lift car. No doubt it had been abandoned far underground and left to rot like everything else in the deserted mine. Stamping his feet up and down, Alfie heard the rattle of the metal telling him he was right. Groping with his hands, he eventually found what had to be an escape hatch on top of the lift, opened it, and leaped down inside. Pushing another huge metal cage door aside, Alfie noticed that far off in the distance there was a glimmer of dim yellow light. Immediately he could make out a few blurred lines among the shadows.

Stepping out, Alfie could feel the cold stone beneath his feet; he was in one of the hundreds of mine tunnels now. There were train tracks running along it. In fact, there were miles and miles of such tracks down here. The miners would have traveled along them to do their work, and sent the mountains of coal back in the mine cars. It was essentially a miniature railway line. With the whole place deserted, they seemed more like the tracks for a ghost train.

At the far end of the tunnel, light was flickering. Alfie walked toward it, slowly and silently. As he grew closer, and shadows danced on the damp walls, he realized this was not electric light, but candlelight. At last he reached the tunnel end, and realized it opened out into a well-lit cave. He peered in.

Nothing could prepare Alfie for what he saw. The cave was vast; it seemed to go on forever. Thousands and thousands of candles illuminated the space.

At first glance there was no sign of Gabz, or the witch and her cat. Dominating the cave was an impossibly long table, but there were no chairs around it. It was white, and looked more like an altar you would see in a church. A plate and a number of goblets adorned the table. All of them white. There was a huge white chandelier hanging down from the ceiling. It held hundreds upon hundreds of candles. On the walls there were mosaics, in the shapes of what looked like prehistoric letters, or some kind of code. Alfie had seen something similar in pictures of the pyramid tombs of ancient Egypt, called hieroglyphics. On one side of the cave sat a huge imposing throne. This again was white. The throne looked big enough for a giant. It was so tall, it reached the ceiling of the cavern.

Was this some kind of temple?

Or a tomb?

Or simply a way of beating skyrocketing house prices?

Tentatively, Alfie stepped inside the cave. He had to find Gabz, and get out of there fast. Running his fingers along one of the mosaics on the walls, looking for any secret doorways, Alfie realized the surface was surprisingly sharp. He cut the tip of one finger open on a particularly sharp bit, drawing blood, but managed to stifle his gasp just in time.

With the blood dripping from his hand, Alfie carefully made his way to the impossibly long table and peered underneath it. Taking a closer look at the tabletop, he realized the whole thing was made up of thousands of tiny fragments. What were they? Very gently he touched it; like the mosaics, it felt uneven and jagged. Intrigued, he picked up the goblet and held it close to his face, examining it in the candlelight. This too was made of countless tiny pieces. Studying it, he finally realized what he was looking at.

The goblet was made up of hundreds of teeth.

Alfie dropped it in horror and it smashed

to the ground. Bending down he picked up some of the little pieces. All of them were teeth. Children's teeth. Just like everything else in the cave—the table, the throne, the chandelier, the goblet. Everything was made entirely of teeth.

The cave was a cathedral of teeth.

A Cateethdral*.

Alfie wanted to scream at the realization, but covered his mouth just in time. How many children in how many towns had suffered just like Alfie, to furnish the witch's lair? It must have been thousands. Tens of thousands, even. Over many years. Perhaps even centuries.

Blinking, Alfie looked to the far side of the cave, where it was deepest in shadow. Squatting there was a huge sooty cauldron, as wide as a paddling pool but much deeper. As he tiptoed over, Alfie realized the cauldron was full of some foul-smelling, thick yellow gunk. A fire

---

Made-up word* **ALERT

was raging underneath. The Tooth Witch was evidently cooking up her special toothpaste mix.

Just then, Alfie thought he saw something moving in the shadows and looked up. Directly above the cauldron a girl was chained by shackles of teeth to some stalactites hanging down from the ceiling of the cave. "Gabz...?" he said.

"Alfie! Is that you?" she whispered. "I couldn't make you out in the dark. I thought you might be the Tooth Witch coming back..."

"No, no, it's me!" he said, drawing closer. "I am here to rescue you!"

"Well, you took your time!" she replied.

"Sorry, it's just...," Alfie spluttered, before realizing he was getting really quite annoyed with her never-ending sarcasm. "Look, do you want to be rescued or not?"

"Shush...," hushed Gabz. "Keep your voice

down! The witch can't be far away..."

"OK, OK," whispered Alfie. "How am I going to get up there to untie you?"

"See if you can drag that throne over here...," she suggested.

"It looks heavy..."

"Well, the witch managed it."

"Yes, but she's a witch and has magical powers."

Gabz gave him a stare, and he realized there was no point arguing. Alfie plodded over to the throne. At first he tried to rock it, but it wouldn't move. Then he put his shoulder up against it. But it just wouldn't budge.

"I'd better run to the bottom of the lift shaft and call up for help," he whispered. "Stay right there..."

Gabz rolled her eyes. "Well, where else do you think I would be going to?"

Alfie tiptoed back to the opening of the cave. But just as he reached it he let out a scream.

"AAAAAAAAAAAA RRRRRRRRRR GGGGGGHH HHHHHHHH!!!!!!!!"

The witch's black eyes were staring right into his. Though her face was upside down. For a moment Alfie was so disorientated he didn't know what was happening. Then he looked up to see she was hanging from the ceiling, like a bat. In her arms she held her cat, Fang, who hissed violently at him.

In that disturbing singsong voice of hers the witch said, "Now be a good boy, Alfie. Come to Mummy..."

34

Look to the Skies

"I knew you would come after us," announced the Tooth Witch in a superior manner. As she spoke, Fang wrapped her tail around her mistress's legs. "You just had to save your little girlfriend..."

"I told you before. She's not my girlfriend!" replied the boy.

Now Alfie was himself chained to the stalactites, next to Gabz. His wrists and ankles were bound by the same manacles, made entirely of teeth. They were actually biting into his skin. It was as if the witch were a spider, and he and Gabz were nothing more than flies caught in her web. Of course, spiders are in no hurry to eat the flies they catch. They like to watch them suffer. The Tooth Witch was no different.

"Well done on your rescue plan...," said Gabz.

"You see, Gabz, that's why I would never go out with you!" replied Alfie. "You are quite pretty but you are actually really annoying."

"You're the annoying one...," replied Gabz.

"Silence, the pair of you!" demanded the witch. "You're both annoying. Getting in the way of my plan to steal all of the children of the town's teeth..."

"Before you boil us, or whatever it is you are going to do," began Gabz, "I would just like to know..."

"Yes, Gabriella, dearest?" the witch sneered.

"What is a Tooth Witch?" asked the girl.

"Yes. Tell us," implored Alfie. "Prove to us you are real..."

"Still you don't believe!" laughed the witch. "How old are you, boy? Eleven?"

"No, I'm twelve," said Alfie indignantly.

"You look younger."

"He is quite short for his age...," agreed Gabz.

"I am actually twelve and a half, nearly thirteen," Alfie snapped.

"Well, children around your age," continued the witch, "twelve and a half, nearly thirteen... you think you know it all. You suppose you're too grown up for stories and myths and legends. You don't want to believe in them anymore. That's why children like you are the easiest to catch..."

"All right, all right...," replied Alfie. "But what's so special about teeth?"

The witch's deep black eyes came flickering to life. "I covet them. Like diamonds or rubies.

I have collected them for centuries. From all over the world. Moving on from place to place. Now I have settled here, and will not rest until every single child's tooth in this town is **mine!**"

The Tooth Witch reached into her pocket, and held one up to the candlelight. "Rotten and decayed ones like yours, Alfie, are the most beautiful. Look at this one. It is perfection. With its gorgeous little nooks and crannies. Look how the light dances on its surface."

"You're nuts!" exclaimed Gabz.

"That'll really help," muttered Alfie.

The witch's eyes narrowed. "If it is 'nuts' to desire teeth, why do the tooth fairies want them so much?"

"But tooth fairies aren't real...," protested the boy.

The witch smiled. "Oh yes, they are.

Annoying little do-gooders flapping all over the place. I think I managed to capture most of the ones flying around this town. They make a tasty treat for Fang here..."

The cat licked her lips.

"OK, so witches and fairies are real. What else?" mused Gabz. "What about Father Christmas?"

Alfie laughed at her. "Gabz! He's not real!"

"Oh yes, he's real all right," replied the witch.

"Yes!" said Gabz triumphantly. "I win!"

"Father Christmas is actually quite a tiresome old codger...," continued the witch. "Going around wishing everyone 'Happy Christmas' all the time. And all those mince pies give him very bad wind. Just don't stand behind him when he bends over to fill a stocking..."

Alfie didn't want his dying thought to be

Father Christmas blowing off, so he quickly moved on.

"But why do you need so many teeth?" he asked.

"So I can build my witch's lair. Every day I need more and more. I have big plans..." The witch became quite animated now. "See that wall?"

The pair nodded.

"Well, I am going to knock through there, and have an extension built, so I can have one big open living space..."

Alfie and Gabz shared a look. They couldn't believe they were chained to the ceiling of a cave listening to a witch's rather tedious home improvement plans.

"You know collecting the teeth has become so easy...," the Tooth Witch continued. "Years ago, witches like me were caught, and drowned in rivers or burned at the stake. But children nowadays don't believe in magic. They are forever watching TV and playing computer games. They never look to the skies anymore. If they did, they would see my cat and me flying about the town at night, going from house to house. Fang here can smell a fresh tooth from miles away..."

The cat hissed in agreement.

"Then we fly down to the child's bedroom window and, without a sound, fly in and snatch the tooth..."

"But why leave those horrible little calling cards behind?" asked Gabz.

The witch smiled. Her pointy fangs glistened in the candlelight.

"Because, child, I am evil. Pure unadulterated evil. That's the really fun part! I put so much effort into those little gifts for the children. Finding the largest cockroach, flattening the toads with a mallet, keeping the pig's eyeballs warm so they are still squirming..."

"You are sick!" shouted Alfie angrily.

“Thank you. And don’t forget twisted. Now, as much as I love compliments I am beginning to tire of our conversation rather…”

The pair gulped in unison. “What are you going to do to us?” ventured Gabz.

“This cauldron is where I boil up ‘MUMMY’S’ special toothpaste…”

“That stuff burns through stone!” said Alfie.

“Yes, the acid in there can destroy anything in its path. If I dunk you both in for just the right amount of time…”

“If you dunk us in, then what…?” asked Gabz nervously.

“It will strip your flesh clean off you…” The Tooth Witch was savoring her words as she spoke, as you or I might savor a particularly delicious flavor of ice cream. “And all that will be left of you will be your bones…”

35

Feasting on Bones

"It is sure to be a slow, agonizing death, children...," expounded the witch, "...exactly how I like them. Then I am going to feast on your bones!"

She looked down at her trusty white cat. "Guess what you are having for tea too, Fang?"

The beast's ears pricked up, and she gazed into her mistress's eyes.

"That's right! Yummy scrummy children's bones..."

Fang purred loudly.

Far off in the distance, Alfie heard an echo. The cat turned her head and hissed. The Tooth Witch cocked her head suspiciously, and then quickened her pace.

With her superhuman strength, she dragged the huge, heavy throne of teeth into position. Next she climbed up to stand on the seat, and started unfastening the chains that bound the children's wrists. Both were now trembling uncontrollably with fear.

"I am going to drop you in the cauldron together," announced the witch, "so you can hear each other's screams as you die..."

"Just to say, I don't mind if you put him in before me...," uttered Gabz, attempting a little black humor to try and lighten the situation.

"Isn't it ladies first?" said Alfie.

Within moments, the witch had untied their wrists. Now the pair were hanging upside down, with the nasty, bubbling yellow gloop lapping at their heads. The noxious stench was so foul Alfie and Gabz could hardly breathe.

"Please, please, please, I beg you…," appealed Alfie now. "You can boil me, but let Gabz go free, she's not done anything wrong…"

It was no use; the witch was not for turning.

"Human emotion. How pitiful…," she muttered as she dragged the throne a few paces and climbed up it again. Now the witch was busying herself unfastening the children's ankles.

"Don't worry, children. Mummy's nearly there. It shouldn't be too long now…," chirped the witch. Alfie's left leg swung free, and his whole body dropped down farther. His hair was now touching the toxic goo below, the acid burning the ends.

Far off, within the depths of the mine, there was a definite sound of something rattling. The witch was struggling with the boy's final manacle. "It's all very well making everything out of teeth, but it does make things very fiddly..."

Now Fang started to help her mistress, leaping onto her shoulder and nibbling at the binds with her sharp teeth.

Any moment now, Alfie was to meet his end.

But looking out into the tunnel that led to the cave, Alfie could just see something traveling fast toward them on the ceiling. In a flash, he realized it wasn't on the ceiling. He was of course upside down. It was on the ground. A train. A train was coming right toward them.

Hanging there like sides of meat at the butcher's, Alfie gave Gabz a look urging her to stay silent. He didn't want them to give the game away to the Tooth Witch. As the train sped toward them, the boy smiled. At the front of it, driving the engine, was a welcome face.

Dad.

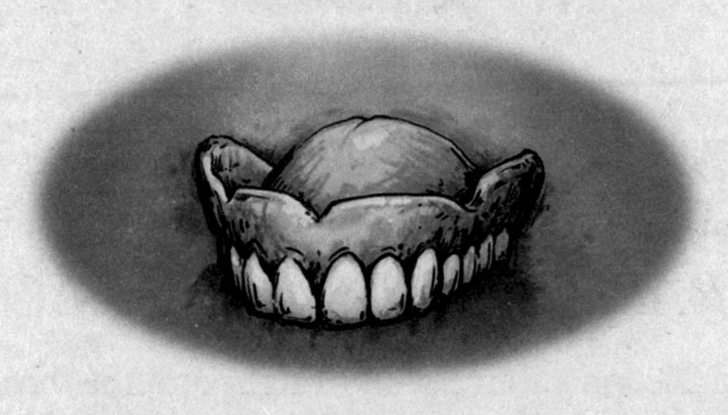

36

Drowning Out Screams

As the clatter of the locomotive became louder, the Tooth Witch turned her head.

"A curse upon you!" she whispered, before hurrying the pace of her wickedness. Her long spindly fingers and Fang's sharp teeth raced to unfasten the boy's final shackle, and plunge him headfirst into the cauldron. As Alfie peered down, he realized he only had seconds to go until he became a skeleton.

The train sped through the entrance of the cave, and careered along its tracks heading straight for the witch. Just as the evil duo had managed to release Alfie's bonds there was a huge ***CRASH***, ***BANG***, and ***WALLOP***, and the locomotive plowed right into the throne. The Tooth Witch lost her balance and she and her feline beast plunged into Mummy's special toothpaste mix.

"AAAAAAAAAAAAA AAAHHHHHHHH!!!!!!!!" screamed the witch.

"Hhhhhiiiiiissssssssssss...!" hissed the cat.

Within moments, both had sunk below the surface, the thick yellow goo drowning out their screams.

Much to his surprise, Alfie was still alive. Gabz had managed to grab his ankle just in time. Now rocking her body back and forth, she swung him clear of the cauldron. It was as if they were a trapeze act at the circus.

As Alfie flew through the air, his dad was just able to grab his wrist, and yank him to the safety of the train. Opening his eyes, Alfie was now clinging by his fingertips to the front of it. Then he turned and looked forward. At that moment he realized he wasn't safe yet.

The train was heading at speed, slap bang into the wall of the cave!

"Dad!" yelled the boy. "The brakes!"

Alfie's father heaved the brake lever up, and with a huge screech the train came to a sudden stop, with Alfie less than a gnat's hair from the rocks.

"Thanks," sighed the boy.

"That's what dads are for…," sputtered his father breathlessly. All the dust and dirt in the cave was no good for his lungs. The doctors had told him never to go back down a mine, that just one more lungful of coal dust could prove fatal. But right now Dad could only think about one thing. Saving his son.

"Dad, you killed the Tooth Witch! And the cat!" exclaimed Alfie.

"All in a day's work...," he joked.

"How did you know I was down here?"

"Winnie called me. She guessed I'd be the only one who knew their way around the mine. And now the whole town is on its way..."

"Good old Winnie...," said the boy.

"Ha hum!" Gabz coughed theatrically.

"Oh yes!" said Alfie. "Sorry, Gabz..."

"Now as much as I normally love hanging upside down over a boiling witch's cauldron, I was wondering whether you could untie me?" she said.

Dad stared at her. "Who's this, son? Your girlfriend?"

"NO! For the last time! She is not my girlfriend!" exclaimed Alfie.

"All right!" replied Dad, coughing quite badly now. "I only asked."

With all his might, he pulled a handle on the engine. Slowly and surely, the train reversed along the tracks to stop beside the cauldron. Alfie leaped off the front and onto the top of the engine. From there he stood on his tiptoes and untied the last of Gabz's manacles. There was a distinctly awkward moment, where Alfie found himself holding the girl who was definitely not his girlfriend upside down by her ankles. However, Dad leaned out and pulled her onto the train. Gabz jumped down, landing on a sack that was sitting in the car behind.

"Careful!" wheezed Dad.

"Why?" asked Gabz.

"That's dynamite!" he replied.

"Cool!" said the girl.

Alfie knew all about how dynamite was used in coal mines. His father had told him many times about how he often needed to blast away hard rock to get to the coal behind.

Gabz's face lit up with an idea. "Let's use the dynamite to seal the cave behind us..."

"The witch is dead!" replied Alfie. "Let's just get out of here!"

And they were about to do just that when...

"Look!" screamed the girl.

Behind them the Tooth Witch and her cat were rising up out of the cauldron. All their skin and flesh had been burned away. Now they were both just skeletons.

Skeletons standing on their bony feet and coming right after them. Fast.

37

Skeletons on the March

The skeletons were marching right toward them. The witch one in front, the cat one a few paces behind, her long thin tailbone standing on end.

"There's no stopping her. Quick! Let's go!" yelled Dad.

Dad yanked the lever, and the train sped backward out of the cave.

Gabz started rummaging through the sack.

"What are you doing?" said Alfie.

"Grabbing the dynamite so we can seal her

in!" replied Gabz. "Now see if you can find a lighter or something..."

Alfie looked under another sack and found a tin housing some ancient matches, then lit the dynamite with shaking hands.

"Be careful, you two!" shouted Dad at the pair.

"Don't throw it until I tell you...," barked the boy.

They both stared nervously at the stick as the fuse burned down. Just before the train reached the cave entrance, Alfie yelled...

"Now!"

The girl threw the dynamite stick into the air and it exploded, bringing huge rocks crashing to the ground behind them. A gigantic cloud of dust and debris filled the tunnel.

"We did it!" cheered Alfie.

Now the train was traveling along the central tunnel at speed. They were heading toward the lift that would take them above ground. And to safety. For a while all that the three could hear was the rattle and hum of the train. Then out of the shadows, Dad spotted something.

"No!" he cried.

The kids turned around and saw the two skeletons, one human and one animal, zooming after them through the tunnel on the gas cylinder.

"Mummy's going to get you...!" screamed the witch-skeleton.

"Dad, make this thing go faster!" shouted Alfie.

"It won't go any faster!" spluttered Dad.

With the cylinder catching up with the train, Fang's skeleton was taking clawed swipes at Dad, who was desperately ducking out of the way.

The witch-skeleton cackled as what was left

of her cat scratched the man's head viciously.

Gabz held the second stick of dynamite, while Alfie lit the fuse.

"Let me throw it this time!" he said.

"Now!" she shouted.

Alfie hurled it at the evil duo hovering just behind them.

KKKKAAAABBBBBOOOOOM!

The explosion threw the pair off balance, but it wasn't enough to stop them dead.

Their bones rattled as they scrabbled to stay on the cylinder.

"We've only got one more stick of dynamite...," warned Gabz.

The cat-skeleton leaped off the cylinder and landed with claws drawn on Dad's head.

"HHHHHHHHHH HHHIIIIIIIIIIIIIIIIIISSSS SSSSSSsssssssssssssss!!!!!!"

She clawed her way over him, until her bum bone was sticking right in the poor man's nose.

"AAAAHHHH!" yelled Dad, as the beast sank her fangs into his arm. In pain, his hand shot up off the train throttle, causing the engine to begin to shudder to a halt. Meanwhile, Alfie had lit the fuse on the last stick of dynamite that Gabz was holding. Just as she was getting ready to throw it...

There was a squeal of brakes as the train stopped dead.

The stick of dynamite slipped out of Gabz's grasp and dropped into the car. The fuse was burning down fast. Any moment now it was going to explode...

38

Mummy's Going to Eat You

"Gabz! Jump!" shouted Alfie. The girl leaped out of the train car. Then the boy vaulted over to his father, and pulled him clear of the engine, just as the dynamite exploded. Rocks fell from the roof of the tunnel, crashing down on top of them. Cat-skeleton retreated to her bony mistress, who had fallen off her laughing gas cylinder some way back down the tunnel. Because of the explosion, the cylinder had sprung a leak. It was hissing on the ground, its sweet-smelling gas filling the mine.

Out of the dust storm behind him, Alfie could see the outline of the witch-skeleton rising to her feet.

The train was now a mangled wreck. And the lift still a long way off. Dad was buried under a mountain of rocks. They had crushed whatever strength he had left in him.

"Run, ha ha, boy!" gasped Dad, as Alfie furiously rolled the rocks off his father's body. "Ha ha! Save yourself! Why am I, ha ha, laughing? This isn't funny! Ha ha!"

"It must be the, ha ha ha, laughing, ha ha, gas!" replied the boy. "I am laughing, ha ha, too! Dad, I am not going to leave you, ha ha, down here. Ha ha! Come on, Gabz, help me, ha ha! Grab an arm! Ha ha ha!"

The kids began to heave Alfie's father down the tunnel.

"I'm, ha ha, too, ha ha, heavy...," wheezed Dad. His breathing was rattling in his chest now. “Leave me, ha ha ha…”

“Never! Ha ha ha!” replied Alfie, and together he and Gabz hauled Dad along the track, closer and closer to the lift.

“Ha ha ha! Mummy’s coming to get you…,” laughed the witch-skeleton, her bones rattling as her shoulders shook. Even what was left of Fang couldn’t stop sniggering. With her super-human strength the witch-skeleton pushed the train and its puny cars aside. Alfie and Gabz started running as fast as they could along the track, dragging Dad behind. Finally, they reached the lift. The man’s wheelchair was lying discarded by the metal door where he must have left it. The three tumbled into the lift, and with all his might Alfie slammed the door shut behind them. The two skeletons had caught up with them now, and soon the bones of their hands and paws were rattling on the door, frantically trying to force it open.

"How did you get the lift working?" pleaded Alfie.

"You just have to connect those two loose wires...," wheezed Dad. "Then pull the top handle..."

Gabz brought the wires together, as Alfie tugged at the lever. The lift shuddered into life. It traveled upward at speed, leaving the evil twosome below. Alfie sighed with relief.

"Dad, we're gonna make it!"

But any relief was short-lived because the skeletons were now clinging on to the caged floor of the lift as it made its ascent. Suddenly the witch-skeleton's long finger bones twisted through the holes in the floor, and grabbed at the children's feet.

A battered and bruised Dad crawled across the floor of the lift. With all the strength he had left in his body, he tried to beat the witch-skeleton's hands back with his fists. However, now she was ripping open the metal floor of the cage, tearing through it like paper. Despite Dad's best efforts, the witch's skull burst through and her razor-sharp teeth bit hard into Gabz's ankles.

"AAAAaaaaaaa aaaaaaaaaaaaa hhhhhhhhhhhhhhh hhhhhhhhhhhhhhh !!!!!!!!!!!!!!!!!!!!!!!!!!!"

screamed the girl.

Clinging on to the bottom of the lift with one bony paw and swiping with the other, Fang the cat-skeleton viciously clawed at Dad's hands. The beast was trying her best to stop him from attacking her mistress. But whatever Dad did, the witch-skeleton would not be deterred anyway. She only tightened her jaws around Gabz's ankle even further before opening them slightly to snarl, "Mummy's going to eat you...!"

39

One Final Breath

Finally the lift jolted to a halt at ground level. Blinking into the daylight, Alfie saw the whole town had now crowded around the entrance to the mine. Winnie was at the front, with Raj cowering just behind her. PC Plank was staring at the scene, his mouth open wide in shock. You could have quite comfortably reversed a riot van into it. Dear Mrs. Morrissey had hobbled over especially, the old lady still apparently on "Special Offer."

Even all the teachers from Alfie's school had raced to see what on earth was going on at the deserted mine. Could there really be a real-life witch on the loose?!

Mr. Snood observed intently, as if the whole thing was a startlingly dramatic "impro." Miss "Knickergate" Hare held tightly on to the arm of the trembling headmaster, in fear that in all the kerfuffle her bloomers might make another appearance. Behind them were the caretaker, the secretary, and a whole horde of pupils. Right at the back was Texting Boy. Though he wasn't really taking any notice as he was busy texting.

When they all saw the witch-skeleton gnawing on Gabz's ankle, everyone gasped in horror. Except Winnie. The fearless social worker bolted forward, and slammed the huge metal lift door open.

"Save the kids...," wheezed Dad. Winnie grabbed Alfie and Gabz, to try and pull them to safety. The boy was dragged clear, but the witch-skeleton had dug her teeth deep into the girl's leg now. And she wasn't letting go.

"Aaaaah!" screamed Gabz. The witch-skeleton's cruel teeth were now gnawing into her bone.

Alfie put his arms round Winnie's waist, and desperately helped her pull.

"Come on, everyone!" implored Raj, as he flung aside his fear and rushed forward to add his weight to the effort to free Gabz. The newsagent grabbed hold of Alfie, and pulled as hard as he could. Then PC Plank sprang into action, then the normally timid Mr. Grey, before all the teachers joined the human chain. Soon everyone was helping in this epic tug of war with the witch-skeleton. Would this demon ever give up…?

Apart from Texting Boy of course. He was still far too busy texting.

Out of the corner of her eye Winnie spotted him. "For goodness' sake, child, put your blasted phone away for a moment!" she boomed. The gormless boy was so startled he immediately put his mobile into his pocket and finally joined in with the pulling.

Together the entire town pulled and pulled and pulled.

"Heave!" cried Winnie. "HEAVE! HEAVE!"

And with one last collective effort, they just managed to pry Gabz free of the jaws of the witch's skull.

The whole town landed on the ground in a giant heap. Squished at the bottom of that giant heap was poor Mrs. Morrissey.

The witch-skeleton, her bony cat now climbing onto her shoulders, had torn more fully through the caged floor of the lift. In a murderous fury, she faced the whole town—her white skull gleaming more than her teeth ever had; the bones of her ribcage throbbing with rage.

"I am going to eat all of your children...boil them alive and feast on their bones!" she roared. The crowd all took a pace back in terror.

Alfie's father was lying motionless on the lift floor. His face was pale and drawn. Now he could hardly breathe. He was in so much pain it was a struggle just keeping his eyes open. Dad had known that if he went down the mine again he couldn't expect to come out alive. He wheezed, and took one final gasp of breath. He stretched up his hand, even that a tremendous effort for him now, and just managed to reach the lift's battered old control box.

"Winnie," he gasped. "Promise you'll look after my little pup for me..."

"Dad!" cried Alfie.

"I love you, son..."

With the very last of his strength, Dad ripped a wire clean out of the control box. The lift remained still for a moment. As if it were floating. Then abruptly it began to plummet down the shaft, taking the witch-skeleton and the cat-skeleton down with it.

"Noooooo!"

screamed the boy, as his dad dropped out of view, but Alfie was helpless to stop it from happening. Winnie grabbed him and held him close. Alfie shut his eyes tightly and buried his head into her chest.

It was the last time he would see his father.

The witch was dead.

But with Dad gone there was to be no celebration.

The man was a hero. He had given his life to save not just his son and Gabz, but all the children of the town. Later that night, when a team of firemen finally made it down to the bottom of the mine shaft to bring back up Dad's body, they found his sacrifice had not been in vain.

The skeletons of the witch and her cat had been crushed to pieces. They were now little more than dust. The children of the town were safe from the Tooth Witch forever.

But there was a terrible price to pay.

One little boy was left an orphan.

40

A Big Comfy Pillow

The sun shone on the day of Dad's funeral. It was a cold winter morning, with frost underfoot. Just a few days before Christmas. The church was packed. Standing room only. Outside the church those who couldn't get in listened to the service via loudspeakers. The whole town had come to pay their respects to this great man.

As the only family member, Alfie would have been alone in the front row of pews, but Winnie sat on one side of him, and directed Raj to sit on the other. The newsagent was first to burst into tears. Winnie passed him a tissue. Being nearly thirteen, Alfie was determined to be strong, but soon his tears came too in huge crashing waves.

The hymns and prayers gave little comfort, but Winnie putting her arm around him did.

With his dad gone, the boy was sure he would never know happiness again. His face soaked with tears, he rested his head on the big comfy pillow that was Winnie. There was no need for words really; all Alfie needed was to be held.

For the past couple of weeks Alfie had been staying at Winnie's flat.

Yes, she wore clothes so multicolored it gave you a splitting headache just to look at them.

Yes, she drove her moped like she was a one-woman motorcycle display team.

Yes, she would always devour the last biscuit.

But slowly and surely, Alfie was growing to love her.

When the funeral service drew to a close, the church gradually began to empty.

"I know your father would have been very proud of you, Alfred," said Raj, as he stroked the boy's hair. "Be strong," he added before bursting into tears again and shuffling out of the church.

During the funeral, Gabz had been sitting in the row of pews behind Alfie. As she left, she leaned forward and whispered in his ear, "We are going to have one hell of a story to tell our children."

Alfie smiled sadly and replied, "They are going to love hearing all about their grandpa, the hero..."

"You bet!" she said, before kissing him tenderly on the cheek and leaving.

Soon Alfie and Winnie were the only two souls left in the church. The boy wasn't ready to go outside and face the crowd of townsfolk just yet. Slowly he reached his hand over to hers, and Winnie held it tight. The pair sat there in silence for a while, as they both sniffed away their tears. Eventually Winnie spoke softly...

"How are your teet?"

"My what?" asked Alfie.

"Your teet!"

"You mean my teeth?"

"Yes. That's what I said." Winnie had arranged for the boy to see a very kindly dentist in the next town. Mrs. Gleam had labored for hours and hours to give Alfie an absolutely perfect set of gnashers.

"They're great. Thanks." He traced his tongue around his shiny new teeth.

"Alfred, as much as I wish I could undo the

past, I can't. Now we must look to the future," said Winnie. "And just before your father died, he asked me to promise him something. Now I know this might not be the right time, but..."

"But...?" asked the boy.

"But at some point," continued Winnie, "we need to talk about who's going to look after you."

"Oh yes," replied Alfie. He was only staying with the social worker for a few weeks. With both his parents gone he would have to be put up for adoption. "Well, Winnie, we might as well talk about it sooner rather than later..."

"Good. Well, as your social worker I've been talking to the adoption agency on your behalf..."

"Yes?" replied the boy.

"And there's quite a few different options, lots of very nice couples out there, who I know would be very lucky to have you, but..." Her sentence trailed off, but she took a deep breath and started once more. By now her voice was cracked with emotion. "Well, I have thought long and hard about what your dad asked me the day he died and..."

"And...?" Was she about to say what he hoped and prayed she would?

"Well...," began Winnie again. This wasn't any easier for her than it was for him. "I was wondering if..." The poor woman was really grasping for her words now. "Well, I was wondering if you might consider letting me adopt you...?"

Alfie smiled, though a tear welled in his eye. Sometimes you can feel happy and sad all at the same time. This was one of those times.

"Oh, Winnie!" he exclaimed. "I was hoping you were going to say that!"

"Well...?" she stammered.

"Yes! Yes! Yes! Of course I would! I love you, Winnie!"

"I love you too, young Alfred!" exclaimed Winnie. She wrapped her big arms around the boy and squeezed him tight, Alfie's face buried deep within her bulk. After a few moments came a voice…

"Sorry. You're squashing me!"

"Oh dear!" said Winnie, as she relaxed her grip a little. "Is that better?"

"Yes," replied Alfie, as he wrapped his arms around her too. "Much better. Much, much better…" No one could replace Dad, but Winnie made him feel safe.

And warm. And most importantly, loved.

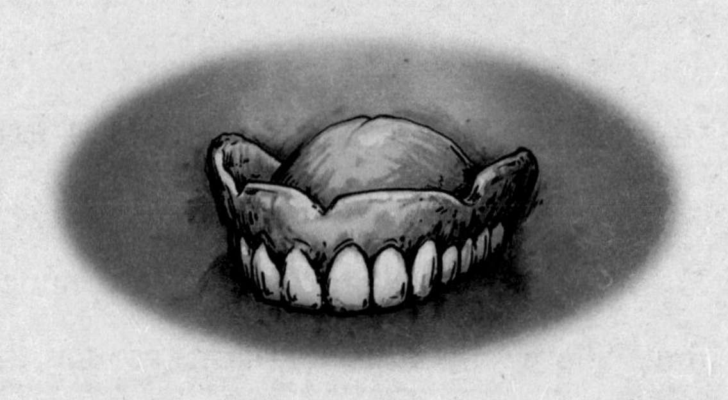

Epilogue

The next time Alfie visited the church, it was a much happier occasion. It was the following year, and much to everyone in the town's surprise, Winnie was finally getting married.

But to whom?

Despite the fact that Alfie was now a teenager, his new mum had asked him to be her page boy. It was a role traditionally reserved for toddlers. Alfie had had no idea what a page boy's duties were, or more importantly what a page boy had to wear. So he had said yes. Little did he know then that Winnie would dress her adopted son in a sailor-themed outfit for her wedding day. Alfie had on a tunic, shorts, knee-high socks and a cap that Winnie insisted should be worn at a "jaunty angle."

Well, thought Alfie, *it is her wedding day...*

However, the boy wasn't the most absurdly dressed person in the church that day. Oh no. And surprisingly, the bride-to-be only made it to second place, despite wearing a dazzling canary-yellow wedding dress, with numerous bustles, layers and a long frilly train. Winnie looked like someone had dipped a hot-air balloon in a giant bucket of custard. But beautiful, in a hot-air-balloony* custardy* type way.

As Winnie walked up the aisle, with her adopted son a few paces behind her carrying

---

Made-up word* **ALERT

her train, the pair saw the groom beaming at the altar.

The man stood waiting proudly for his beautiful bride-to-be, munching on an out-of-date toffee. Yes, the town's most eligible bachelor had found love again...

Raj!

The newsagent would have easily won a prize for being the most absurdly dressed person at a wedding. Ever. Winnie had kitted him out for their special day in a bright purple top hat and tails. Raj's outfit was what a comedy penguin might wear on a mid-price greetings card.

It was Alfie who had brought them together. He would often ask his new mum to stop off at Raj's little shop on the way home from school. Over all the crazy special offers and out-of-date chocolates, the unlikely pair had fallen in love.

Both Winnie and Raj had lived alone for

many years. Although neither had children, both dearly wanted to be parents but assumed the opportunity had passed them by forever. Fortunately they were very much mistaken. Now they were going to be part of a loving family. With Alfie at the center of it.

"Do you, Winnie Prophecy Mystelle Passionfruit Turquoise Dave Smith, take this man to be your husband…?" recited the vicar. He looked more than a little concerned that the list of Winnie's middle names would never end.

"I do," boomed the bride.

"And do you, Raj…?" The vicar stopped. Surely the newsagent had at least a surname?

"No, vicar, it's just Raj…," chirped the groom.

The vicar continued. "Do you, Raj, take this woman to be your wife?"

"Is this the bit where I say 'I do'?" asked Raj. Winnie rolled her eyes.

"Yes!" she barked.

Raj looked at his beautiful bride with great love in his eyes, before replying, "I do."

"Then I now pronounce you man and wife," concluded the vicar. "You may kiss the bride."

The unlikely pair of lovebirds kissed.

When they finally parted, some of Winnie's mandarin-colored lipstick was smeared all over Raj's mouth. It looked like the newsagent had been sucking greedily on one of his own ice lollies. The newly married couple turned to face the congregation, who applauded wildly at this happy union.

No one louder than Alfie. Now he could have all the free sweets in the world. Well, all the out-of-date ones at least.

Outside the church the confetti was thrown, and the photographs taken.

All that was left was for Winnie to throw her wedding bouquet over her shoulder. Folklore said that whichever woman caught it would be next to be married. As Miss Hare, Mrs. Morrissey, and all the unmarried maids of the town circled behind the bride, Winnie flung her spray of flowers high into the air. Without her even attempting to catch it, the bouquet landed squarely on Gabz's head. The girl, who wasn't quite so little anymore, laughed and smiled over at her boyfriend. Alfie smiled back. *Maybe one day we will…*, he thought.

Soon it was time for the bride and groom to leave for the honeymoon, and Winnie straddled her moped. There was a "Just Married" sign stuck on the back, and the small vehicle trailed cans on string, as is traditional for the wedding vehicle.

"Come on, husband!" she cooed. Raj took a running jump and leaped on the back.

"And come on, Alfred!" said Raj.

"Yes, come on, pup…," called Winnie. Alfie hopped on between them, before the three tutted away on the tiny moped, its engine struggling under their considerable combined weight.

"Hold on!" said Winnie, as she threw the bike into a wheelie outside the church to delight the congregation, before righting it again and whizzing off down the road.

Sandwiched between Winnie and Raj, and with the warm summer wind blowing on his face, Alfie couldn't help but smile. The day his father died, Alfie thought any chance he had of ever being happy again had died too. However, as they zoomed through the town and off into the distance, he closed his eyes. He wanted to catch this feeling. Happiness.

In his head, Alfie could hear Dad's voice.

"All you have to do is close your eyes, and believe…"

Thank yous:

A few very impootment* thankingyous*.

Thankingyou* to the head of children's books at HarperCollins, Ann-Janine Murtagh, for all your beliefmentness* in me and my boovels*.

The editor Ruth Alltimes must be thankinged* too for her meticuliffilous* editnessment*.

Kate Clarke and Elorine Grant, thankingyou* both for your incrediment* cover and text designyness*.

The publicimitiousness* for this boovel* was organmented* by Sam White and Geraldine Stroud, thankingyou* ladymen*.

Thankingyou* too to the desk editor Lily Morgan.

Finallingness*, a hugalumptious* thankingyou* to my agent Paul Stevens at Independent. You are the bestmentiousness*.

---

* *Multiple made-up word and phrase* **ALERTS**